COURAGEOUS

COURAGEOUS

A NOVEL OF DUNKIRK

YONA ZELDIS MCDONOUGH

SCHOLASTIC PRESS / NEW YORK

Library of Congress Cataloging-in-Publication Data available

ISBN 978-1-338-22685-0

10 9 8 7 6 5 4 3 2 1   18 19 20 21 22

Printed in the U.S.A.   23

First edition, December 2018

Book design by Yaffa Jaskoll

For Paul, who still loves a great adventure story

ONE

Aidan looks up. The sky that had been blue and cloudless only minutes ago is now dark and menacing. If it starts to rain, and it looks like it will, he'll be soaked because his yellow mackintosh is at home, on the hook by the door, and not here in the dory with him.

The wind picks up, rocking the small boat from side to side and blowing a fine, cold spray in his face. Aidan holds on tightly, but the angry, churning sea and its foam-capped waves are tossing the poor little dory mercilessly. A big wave smacks up and over the side, and in an instant, Aidan is soaked. Water pools on the dory's deck, making the boat even less seaworthy than it had been.

With a rush, the rain that has been threatening suddenly floods from the sky. The waves grow stronger and Aidan's stomach lurches as the next big swell capsizes the small vessel and he is plunged, sputtering and kicking, into the cold gray sea. He tries to reach for the overturned dory but another wave yanks it away. He is alone here in the dark, roiling ocean. He tries to scream, to cry for help, but the words seem jammed in his throat and when he opens his mouth nothing comes out. With horror, he looks up to a wall of water, a wave larger and more ferocious than any that have come before. In seconds it will break, and when it does, it will engulf him completely, and pull him down, down, down—

With a start, Aidan bolts upright in bed. His pajama top is soaked in sweat, and his heart is throbbing. It was the dream—again. He takes three deep breaths, exhaling slowly after each one. He's found that counting the breaths helps him calm down. Then he hears a thud and he jumps a little before he realizes that it's just Maude, the ginger cat, landing on the floor. She seems to sense his distress, because she leaps up onto the bed, plants herself under Aidan's outstretched hand, and begins to purr.

"Good kitty," he murmurs. His heart slows and he settles back into bed, glancing at the window. The sky is still dark and he wonders if he'll be able to get back to sleep. The cat's continued purring calms him though, and he settles back into the pillow. He prays the dream won't come again—at least not tonight.

Several hours later, Aidan wakes again. The cottage is quiet, so he decides he's probably the first one up. He dresses quickly, then reaches for his cap, his jacket, and his fishing rod. He eases the door open, careful not to let the hinges squeak. Once he's outside the cottage, he sets out down the road, toward the dock. It's early on a morning in late May and the sky is just beginning to lighten. He can hear the birds gently chattering in the trees, and he sees a streak of brown—a small brown rabbit darting across his path.

Aidan's been taking this walk since he was a little kid. He can remember walking hand in hand with his dad through the dawn, the smell of the sea so fresh, so bracing, and growing stronger as they approached the water. His older brothers, Trevor and George, would be walking up ahead, chasing each other and laughing as they went. Dad would tell them to settle down, but he was always smiling when he said it. He smiled a lot back then. But that was before the war. Before Trevor's navy boat exploded and he was drowned in the Atlantic Ocean. Before George went off to fight in France.

Aidan tries not to think about the day the telegram came, but he knows he'll never be able to forget it either. Mum went white even before she read it; she thrust it into Dad's hands, as if she were unable to be the first to know. Dad's eyes filled with tears and he made strange, huffing sounds like he was having trouble breathing. Aidan knew something terrible had happened even before the awful details were revealed. Trevor's boat had been struck by a U-boat one night while most of the men were sleeping. They'd been caught by surprise, and later Aidan's parents learned that all but one of the crew had been killed. Now, Dad walks around with a tight, grim expression all the time, and

Mum's eyes look haunted, even when she smiles, which is hardly ever. And Aidan is haunted each night in his dreams.

Soon, Aidan reaches the dock, where he can see his family's wooden dory bobbing gently on the waves alongside a couple of rowboats, the blue-and-white boat owned by Mr. Potts, and the smart yellow boat that belongs to Mr. Aspern, who hardly ever takes it out. The dory is eighteen feet long, painted red, and has the name *Margaret* in white script along the side. Margaret's his mum's name, though Dad always calls her Peggy.

No one else is here at the water yet. Aidan gets into the dory, unties the rope, lifts the anchor, and turns on the engine. He's shivering a little—even for England, it's been an unusually wet, cold spring—and he wishes he'd put a sweater on under his light jacket. As he guides the wheel, the heaviness in his chest begins to ease. The ocean's always been his friend. The pull of the tides, the cries of the gulls overhead, the sunlight glinting on the foam-tipped waves—all these things have been a part of him forever.

But ever since Trevor was killed, Aidan's felt afraid of the ocean. Afraid of its depth. Its power. The ocean is his brother's grave—his body was never recovered. And though Aidan doesn't like to admit his fear, he's been secretly afraid that the ocean will claim him too. He thinks that must be why he has those terrible dreams—because of his fear.

He has to stop thinking like this. He continues to steer the boat and when he's out far enough, he turns off the engine, picks up the rod, and reaches into the bait barrel. It's nearly empty. Usually, Dad sees to getting it filled but clearly he's forgotten, so Aidan reminds himself to take care of refilling the barrel once he's back on shore. When he's baited the hook, he casts his line out into the sea. Dad usually uses nets to catch fish, but Aidan's not planning to be out here for very long and he doesn't want to bother.

For a long while, there is nothing—not a tug, not a pull, not a nibble. Aidan's not worried though. His father taught him that a good fisherman needs patience. "The ocean has its own rhythms," he said. "The fish bite when they bite." Only, Dad's not doing much fishing these days. Instead, he's spending time at the local pub, hunched over a glass of ale that he nurses for hours. Last night he didn't even come home for dinner, and Aidan sat across from Mum in sorrowful silence, the empty chairs at the table a reproach and a wound.

Still, Aidan is out here today, even if his father isn't. *Someone* in this family needs to catch some fish, and it looks like he's the one. When he feels the line go taut, his instincts, honed from years of experience, instantly kick in. He knows just when to let the line go slack, and just when to pull. And he's rewarded, a few minutes later, with a flat white flounder flopping around the bottom of the boat. Gutted and deboned, it would make a delicious meal of Dover sole. But Aidan knows Mum's not likely to make such a meal anytime soon. Ever since Trevor died, Mum seems like a sleepwalker. She spends hours in front of the window, just looking out. He thinks regretfully of the fish dinners she used to prepare. Then there were the scones, the jam tarts, and, on special occasions, the trifles piled high with custard, cream, and berries. His stomach rumbles just thinking about it, and he realizes that he forgot to take any breakfast before he left.

Aidan remains on the water for another hour or so, but the fish are sluggish, and he only manages to catch three more. One is so puny that he tosses it back in disgust. If Trevor had caught a fish this small, he'd make a big show of pretending he was going to take it home and turn it into a pet. That was Trevor, all right—he could make a joke of anything. George was always the serious, studious one. Before the war, their parents had talked of his going to university, where he wanted to pursue chemistry. Not so for Trevor, who didn't care much for studying, books, or classrooms. But he was always so merry, so good-natured and full of fun that his teachers loved him anyway. Everyone did.

Trevor honed his skills for doing card tricks and juggling. He rode his bicycle on a single wheel, whirled their mum around the kitchen in a silly dance, sang loudly at any chance he got, always had the lead in the school play and the Christmas pageant. And now he's gone, his energy, wit, and spirit extinguished like a blown-out candle. Some days, Aidan believes he'll be able to accept his brother's death. Other days, he fears he never will.

Dejected and hungry, Aidan decides to head back to shore. He looks at the first flounder he caught, the largest of the catch, and thinks again of the tasty meal it would make. But if he brings it home, it may well go to waste—best not to bother.

At the dock, Aidan stops at the shack run by Mr. Deards. "Not biting today, are they, lad?" says Mr. Deards.

"No, sir," replies Aidan.

"That's all right. Tomorrow will be better."

Will it? Aidan wants to say. But he keeps quiet while Mr. Deards weighs his catch and hands him a few coins in exchange. Aidan uses one of them to buy bait for the barrel. Then he deposits the slimy, smelly fish heads in the bait bucket and heads back down the road, coins jingling softly in his pocket. The sun is higher in the sky now and the day is actually warm, so he takes off his jacket and ties it around his waist. Soon he's back home again. But the cottage looks dark and unwelcoming, and he continues on beyond it, down the road to the cottage of his best friend, Sally.

The door to the Sparks cottage is wide open when he arrives, and out front he sees Sally's mum, beating a rug with a wire beater in the spring sunshine.

"Morning, Aidan!" she calls out. "Have you eaten yet?"

"No, ma'am," he says.

"You must be starved. Go inside and help yourself to a bun. Or two. And some tea."

Tea and buns sound just about right, and he's thinking about how good those buns will taste as he walks in the cottage door. Stepping inside, he nearly collides with Sally. She's almost a head taller than he is, with a friendly, freckled face and wild golden hair that resists any attempt to tame it. They were born within a week of each other and have been friends forever.

"There you are!" she exclaims. "I've been looking all over."

"For me?" Aidan snags a bun from the table and takes a big bite—it's delicious, and still warm from the oven.

"Are you daft? Who else? I've got *news*."

"What is it?" He's hungry, all right, but he's more interested in what Sally has to tell him.

"I heard—" Her gaze moves to the door, which is still open. "Let's go to the lighthouse. No one will bother us there." Sally's dad is the lighthouse keeper and she's allowed inside whenever she wants. And because Aidan is her best friend, he's allowed to go with her.

"Okay." He crams a second bun into his mouth. Tea will have to wait. Then he's following Sally outside, down the road and back toward the pebbled beach, where the red-and-white lighthouse stands proudly against the sky. Together they climb the narrow, winding stairs until they reach the top, a light-filled room with windows all around. There's a desk, a couple of wooden chairs, a coal stove, and a table. But Aidan doesn't care about any of that. His eyes go straight for the radio he and Sally have managed to assemble.

Sally had helped Mrs. Leeds clean out her cellar, and Mrs. Leeds let Sally take the broken radio that had been collecting dust on one of the shelves. Over a period of weeks, Sally and Aidan have managed to get it working again, even if it's a makeshift thing, held together with tape, assorted wires, some tubes Sally scrounged, and even a little bit of chewing gum. Amazingly enough, it works, and on a clear night, it can pick up signals all the way from Dover.

"Did you hear something?"

She nods. "That's why I came looking for you."

"Well, what is it?"

"It was in code, so I couldn't be entirely sure. But I kept hearing this word *dynamo*. What do you suppose that is?"

"I haven't a clue," says Aidan.

"Me neither."

"And they kept talking about the coast too. Like it was important."

They are silent for a moment, and Aidan thinks back to the last letter that came from George. *I've got to be brave,* he'd written. *We all do. My mates think the worst is yet to come.*

His mum had looked positively ill when she read those words aloud but his dad tried to minimize the danger they suggested. "The trouble's mainly up north, in London," he'd said. "And in Paris too. Georgie says he's somewhere in the French countryside. He'll be all right."

Maybe his dad was wrong though. Maybe the coded message Sally heard is saying something else.

". . . so stay over tonight, can you?" Sally was saying. "We'll come down to the lighthouse and listen again. Then we can figure out what it all means."

Aidan takes in her wide, frightened blue eyes, and the serious set of her mouth. "Not just what it *means,*" he says grimly. "We have to figure out what we can *do.*

TWO

Aidan leaves Sally's place and heads home, where he finds his mum with her arms elbow-deep in sudsy water, doing the washing up. His dad has already left— for the dockside or the pub, Aidan doesn't know.

"Your father was looking for you," says his mum. "He's gone out on the boat."

Well, that's an improvement, Aidan thinks. He's relieved that his dad is fishing again and is sorry he didn't wait so they could have gone together. That would have been nice. "I was out earlier," he says. "Here's the money from what I caught. It wasn't much." He puts the coins on the table.

"Every bit helps." His mum smiles and ruffles his hair with her hand, something she hasn't done in a while. The gesture used to annoy him because he thought she was treating him like a baby. Now he's just glad that she's acting more like her old self. She fixes him a cup of tea, and even though he had those buns at Sally's, he eats the porridge she spoons into a bowl. Then he heads back down to the water and waits anxiously for the dory to return.

The dock is more active now, with a handful of boats out on the water and others coming in, their nets filled with wriggling, gleaming fish. He sees Ned Blarry and Herb Whitson, men who have fished with his father for years. Ned carries a big coil of rope on his shoulder and Herb's got a bait bucket, battered and scarred by decades of use. "Hey, Aidan," Ned calls. "What's the news from George?"

"Not so good." Aidan walks over to join the men. "We had a letter from him. He thinks the worst is yet to come."

Ned and Herb exchange looks.

"Your dad wouldn't say but we see it in his eyes," Herb says. "He's already lost a boy and he's worried sick about Georgie. So are we—he's one of our own."

"That's how it is with all you boys," says Ned. "We've seen you born and watched you grow—you too, lad. And then sometimes, we have to watch you die, like Trevor, may he rest in peace."

Aidan is shocked for a moment. People don't usually bring up the subject quite so plainly. Then he realizes he's grateful that Ned has said his brother's name. It's not only a way to remember and honor him. It's a way to keep his spirit alive.

". . . and if there's anything we can do," Herb is saying. "You'll let us know, won't you?"

"I will," says Aidan. "And thank you kindly." Aidan's grateful for their concern but really, what can they do? What can anyone, for that matter? Except that he and Sally are going to try to do . . . something, though it's not clear what.

A short while later, the *Margaret* pulls up to the dock. Aidan waves and watches as his dad switches off the engine and ties the boat to the wooden piling. Then Aidan hops aboard. He and his dad spend the rest of the afternoon making a few small repairs. His dad doesn't say much while they work, but Aidan's glad to be in his company, and to have something useful to do. It helps make the time until this evening go faster.

They finish up around six o'clock and when they get back to the cottage, Aidan is surprised to find that his mum has prepared fish stew for dinner. When she takes the cover off the pot, the rich, enticing aroma fills the room. And after he's washed up and they all sit down to eat, he's even more pleased to find she's baked rolls to go with it.

"This is delicious, Mum," Aidan says, helping himself to another serving.

"Thank you," says his mother. "I know it's one of your favorites."

It was Trevor's favorite too. Aidan doesn't want to say that. If he does, he'll ruin everyone's mood. So instead, he says, "I was going to spend the night at Sally's. Her mum says it's all right." He bites into the roll.

"Just be back in time for church tomorrow," his

mum says. "We're all going to go together—we need to pray for George."

"It's going to take more than prayers, Peggy," says his dad.

"Well, prayers can't hurt." His mum gets up from the table abruptly. Aidan sighs. So the mood is ruined after all, even if he wasn't the one to ruin it. He continues eating, but somehow the food has lost a bit of its savor, and he guesses that if he looks at his mum's face, he'll see there are tears coating it.

It's still light when he heads down to Sally's house. She's waiting for him outside, and they walk down to the lighthouse, which is in the opposite direction from the dock and just a short distance from her place. The wind has picked up and the white-foamed waves, though small, break with surprising force against the rocks. The friends go into the lighthouse and climb the circular stairs up to the top. "My dad will be here soon," Sally says as they climb. "I don't want him to know what we're up to. So we can't stay that long."

"Then let's get started right away," says Aidan. He

switches on the radio they have built, and at first they hear only static. But Sally's good with the radio—she did most of the building. She fiddles with the dials, adjusting them back and forth, and soon they hear some German voices, rapid-fire and loud. Neither Sally nor Aidan understands German, so most of what they hear is incomprehensible. But there is one word they *do* understand. *Dunkirk*. Isn't that just a little French town on the other side of the English Channel? Aidan is pretty sure George is somewhere near there. Anyway, it's been repeated several times, so it must be important. Now they just need to find out why. "Why do you suppose they keep mentioning Dunkirk? Is something going to happen there?" Sally asks.

"It could be an invasion," Aidan ventures. "Or maybe it's a defensive position."

"Nothing defensive about the Germans right now," says Sally. She's right. The Germans are getting stronger every day. In fact, they seem invincible. Their early, easy victories—in Austria, Poland, France, Belgium,

Luxembourg, and the Netherlands—make them seem almost superhuman, on the march and on the rise.

Sally keeps turning the dial, and soon she's found an English-speaking station. "... the government is getting ready to requisition civilian ships to aid in the war effort..." But a burst of static interrupts the broadcast, and the rest of the words are lost.

As Sally tries to adjust the dial, a noise on the stairs makes them both fall silent. She quickly switches off the radio as her father walks into the room. "I wondered where you kids ran off to," he says. "I should have guessed."

"You know we just like it up here, Dad," Sally says. "Looking out over the water. The view's grand and..."

"Right," says her father, glancing at the radio. "And then there's that thing you two managed to cobble together. Pretty clever, I must say. Does it actually work?"

"Sort of..." says Sally. "Not all of the time though."

"And what do you hear? Secret messages from the other side? Cracking the German codes, are you?"

Aidan can tell he's just joking—he has no idea of what they've been able to hear. But Sally looks nervous, so Aidan jumps into the conversation to rescue her. "Even if we did hear something, it would be nothing but gibberish to us, sir," he says. "Sally and I don't understand a word of German."

"Not many of us do," says her father, suddenly serious. "I just hope and pray that we're not going to be *forced* to understand it one day." He sighs and sits down at the desk.

On the other side of the Channel, somewhere in a little French village not far from the coast, Aidan's brother George is sound asleep. So deeply asleep that he doesn't hear Commanding Officer Rogers's barked orders, and it's not until another soldier gives him a less than gentle shove that he reluctantly opens his eyes.

"Get a move on, mate!" says the soldier who shoved him.

"What for?" George wants nothing more than to go back to sleep. They were up almost all of last night, marching to this nameless little village, and it's only been an hour or two at most since he tumbled into bed—or the stiff, unyielding cot that passes for a bed.

"Didn't you hear? CO's just said we're to pack up. We're headed for Dunkirk."

"Dunkirk?" asks George. "Why there?" He's familiar with the name—it's a coastal town and has some strategic importance. But why now when they've only just arrived here and are all so desperate for a few hours of sleep?

"Haven't you learned anything yet, mate?" The other soldier looks at him pityingly. "There's no point in asking why. Just obey orders and make it snappy."

"Can't we sleep a little longer?" George says. "An hour. A half hour even."

"Orders are orders," says the soldier.

So George reluctantly pulls himself up and begins to gather his few belongings. By the time he falls into line to begin the march, he's fully awake and wondering what they'll find at Dunkirk. Only now, he doesn't even bother to ask—he just does what he's told.

"One, two, three, four." They march down the road for two hours, but it might as well be two days. It starts to rain, a chilled, stinging rain more suited to November than late in May, and to George it feels like it will be raining forever. He's discovered that there's a hole in the sole of his left boot, and every time he takes a step, a nasty mixture of cold water and mud squirts inside. His foot makes squelching sounds as he marches. Not only that, he now feels like he's coming down with a sore throat and his head is so heavy it feels like it's filled with rocks. His clobber bag feels like it's full of rocks too, even though he knows it's his clothes, his shaving gear, a book, and a dented tin of biscuits that are making it such a burden.

George struggles to keep pace but it's hard with that hole, the heavy clobber, and the persistent throbbing in his head. What he wouldn't give to get out of this cursed rain, and to be sitting by a crackling fire with a hot mug of tea in his hand—

"One, two, three, four!" The sharp voice of the CO breaks into George's reverie and he refocuses his attention on the present. The village they're now marching through seems like a ghost town: There's no one around, and the cottages are all shut up and dark. Well, no wonder, with the Germans swarming through the countryside, gobbling up everything in their path. He begins to pay closer attention to the buildings as a way of staying alert: cottage, cottage, barn, cottage. There's something up ahead that looks like a school, and beyond that a church. Then another scattering of cottages and a barn, this one quite large, its once-red paint faded to a soft, muted pink.

For some reason, his eye lingers on this barn for a little longer than the other buildings he's passing. Maybe it's because of the handsome black horse extending his powerful neck out of the opening to his stall, the only sign of life George has seen in this desolate little village. And it's in that second that he sees it, slow like in a dream: the shadowy figure just behind the horse, the raised arm. But that mere second or two spells the difference between life and death.

"Take cover!" George shouts at the top of his lungs, and with a strength he's not aware he has, he shoves the two men closest to him, just in time. There's a flash and burst of fire as a grenade explodes practically in front of him. He can feel the heat from the fire that flares suddenly and then sputters in the rain, and the brightness blinds him for a few seconds.

When his eyes clear, George cautiously gets to his knees, keeping his head down. Apart from being coated in mud, he's all right. And so, apparently, are the two mates he shoved into the mud with him. He knows because he can hear them exclaiming, "He's in the barn! It's Jerry"—that's what they call the German soldiers—"he's in there!"

There are a few seconds of confusion as someone gives the order to fire and the shooting begins, a deafening *rat-tat-tat* of machine guns. The horse utters a panicked whinny and retreats into the recesses of the barn as the men rush toward it. George can't tell what's going on in the noise and rain—and suddenly everything is strangely, eerily silent. Their attacker was just a lone German soldier.

The other soldiers swarm around the man's corpse, arguing over who will get his boots, his gun, his jacket, which is in good shape and made of wool. George climbs to his feet and helps pull upright the men he knocked over. Rogers walks over, claps him on the back, and says, "Right, good work," and the two men who had been on either side of him grab his hands and raise them up in the air, a victory pose.

"Thank you, sir," George manages to say.

He badly wants to spit the mud from his mouth but he waits until Rogers has resumed his place at the head of the unit. The other men are still tussling over the German's possessions, and finally they get it all sorted out and they file back to re-form their lines. Something small and blue catches George's eye and before anyone can say anything, he darts over and scoops it up. No one even notices. It's some kind of leather wallet, but there's no time to look at it now. He decides he'll save it for later, when he's by himself.

Rogers gives the order and the unit continues its march. It's still raining, but George is no longer tired and, amazingly enough, his head no longer throbs. His eyes seek out the opening of the stall. There is no horse visible and this makes him inexplicably sad. He wishes he could run into the barn and see if the beautiful animal is all right but of course he can't. So he marches alongside his comrades, and when they break into a rousing fight song, he lets his voice rise up to mingle with theirs.

Later, when they've stopped for a break, George takes the opportunity to move away from the group. Turning his back to shield what he's doing, he pulls out the blue leather wallet he found earlier.

Inside, he discovers a few German deutsche marks, some kind of identification card, two photographs, and, tucked deep inside a corner of the wallet, a bit of red ribbon. He looks at the ID first. Gerhardt Lieber, born

January 5, 1922. That means he is—or was—eighteen, a year younger than George. There's a picture of him dressed in a knit cap and parka, holding a pair of skis in one hand, his other arm draped casually around the shoulders of a pretty girl. Is she his sister? No, she looks more like his girlfriend. She's smiling, and has braids poking out of her own knit cap. The braids are tied with ribbons. Red ribbons, like the frayed bit in the wallet? George can't be sure from the photo.

The other picture is of a middle-aged man and woman in good clothes, standing in front of a solid-looking brick house with flowers by the door. Are they Gerhardt's parents? And is that his house, the one in which he grew up and to which he'll never return?

"What's that you've got there?"

Startled, George looks up to see Clarence Ivers, who has the annoying habit of nosing into everyone's business.

"Nothing," says George, and he quickly stuffs everything into his pocket.

"You look pretty interested in . . . nothing," Clarence says.

George walks away to join the others. He'd like to spend more time examining the contents of the wallet, but even after just a single look, he feels that he knows a few essential things about Gerhardt. He was eighteen and liked to ski. He was sentimental enough to keep a picture of his parents and his sweetheart in his wallet when he went off to war. That middle-aged couple—how they will grieve when they get the news about their boy, just like his mum and dad did when they got the news about Trevor. And the girl with the braids—she'll cry too. War leaves everyone crying, he realizes. There's no way around it. Every single man, on either side of the fighting, is loved and cherished by people back home—wherever home happens to be. And the loss of any life, anywhere, leaves a terrible hole in the hearts of all those people who are left behind.

*　*　*

Sally must have fallen asleep as soon as her head hit the pillow, because even from his little room across the hall, Aidan can hear when she starts to snore. But he remains awake and restless, with the word *Dunkirk* beating a disturbing refrain in his mind. He knows it's a port town on the other side of the Channel, and because it's a port, it's a strategic city for the Germans to capture. Is that why they were talking about it? Or maybe something else is going to happen at Dunkirk? From the excited sound of those voices, Aidan imagines that it must be something of great importance. He thinks again about George and hopes his brother is nowhere near Dunkirk.

Finally, just before dawn, he falls into a light, restless sleep. The dream comes to him again, and he feels the familiar terror as he crashes into the sea and gazes up at the forty-foot wall of water before him. He wakes, and the fear recedes, replaced by relief. Yes, it was awful. But it was just a dream.

Aidan dresses in a hurry. He'll come back to see Sally later, but right now, he's got to get to church.

He's promised his mum that he'll be there, and more than anything, he doesn't want to let her down. Lord knows she's had enough sadness in the last months, and he's not going to add to it, even with a little thing like missing church. Aidan knows his dad's faith has been shaken, that he questions what he's believed in his whole life long. Mum is different though. Hope is still alive in her, and Aidan realizes, with great clarity, that he wants to be like his mum in this way and not like his dad. He wants to keep hope alive—hope that his brother, and all the other English boys with him, will stay safe and return to the families they love, the families that are just waiting for them to come home.

THREE

The church service, led by Reverend Blake, is unusually subdued. So many of the town's boys are overseas fighting against the Germans, and the villagers know they are lucky to be alive to fight, since many of their comrades are not.

When it is over, Aidan files out quietly with his parents.

The rest of the day is slow and still, all the shops closed, though the pub is open. Aidan's father doesn't go out fishing on Sundays and neither does Aidan. And he doesn't go with his father to the pub either. Mum serves the stew again for supper but that's all right. Aidan's just glad to have a hot meal at home two days in a row, since neither of his parents have acted much like themselves lately. In the evening, they gather round the radio for the news. Aidan is on the alert for any mention of Dunkirk, but there is none.

The next day, he heads off to school, where he meets up with Sally and some of their other friends—Aggie, Isabel, Mikey, and Bradford. There's the familiar routine of maths and history in the morning, writing and grammar in the afternoon. There's a weak bit of sun struggling to get through the clouds, and the May afternoon is, if not warm, at least not chilly. After school Aidan joins a game of football. At this moment, in their quiet little seaside village, Aidan can almost let himself believe that everything is all right.

But as soon as Aidan gets home, that illusion is shattered. Both of his parents are sitting in the parlor, and the radio is blaring its news loudly. They neither speak nor move, and their faces are ashen. And they barely even look over when he comes in. Their eyes remain fixed on the radio, as if it can offer them images to go with the words.

Aidan drops his satchel and plants himself on the floor, right next to the radio. The announcer's somber voice prompts the panic he sees reflected on the ashen faces of his parents.

". . . the Second Panzer Division rolled on, covering forty miles in fourteen hours. In a single, massive stroke, they cut the Allied forces in two. The BEF, two French armies, and all the Belgians—nearly a million men—are now sealed in Flanders, pinned against the sea and ready for taking."

"Turn it off," says Aidan's mother. "Please, turn it off."

Aidan's father does as she asks and now the room is filled with a silence even more awful than the BBC announcer's words.

"George is a member of the BEF," Aidan says quietly. It's too awful to think of—George and his mates, surrounded, trapped and at the mercy of their enemies.

"That he is," says Aidan's father. His mother says nothing but gets up and quietly leaves the room.

"What will happen to George, Dad?" asks Aidan when they're alone.

"I wish I knew," says his father. "Maybe Mum is right—we do have to keep praying for him. And hope our prayers can keep him safe."

Aidan had been in church with his parents and seen the grave expressions on faces all around him. Dad was right the first time—they need more than prayers. But what?

At school that week, everyone is talking about the stranded boys. Aidan is not the only one with a family member in danger. So many of his schoolmates have brothers, cousins, uncles who have been called up for duty. Even the teachers are not exempt. One has a son who is in the army, and another a husband. Some people are even saying that the government is going to ask for help from civilians. Isn't that what he and Sally heard on the radio the other night? Aidan thinks about what this could mean. People back home were already helping by accepting the rationing of food and other resources and by knitting socks and caps for boys. What else could they be doing?

After chores are finished on Saturday, Aidan and Sally hurry down to the lighthouse and go straight for the radio. There is the usual static as they try to get a clear signal, but today the static doesn't resolve as quickly as it usually does. "I think there's a problem," says Sally. "Maybe it's this tube here . . ."

Aidan watches while she disconnects one tube after another, seeking to find the source of the trouble. He's a little bit in awe of her skills in this department. She just seems to know what to do, and even when she doesn't, she can puzzle it out. And after about fifteen minutes, she's fixed the radio.

Eagerly, they return to the dials in an effort to get a clear signal. Today they home in on something new and startling: The government is about to ask that all civilians living along the coastline of the

Channel—Dover, Kent, Deal, and others—bring their boats to Dunkirk, to ferry the stranded men to safety. Fishing boats, yachts, sailboats, tugboats—every boat on the English coast is needed. Tomorrow, the little boats are going to start making their journeys and Operation Dynamo will officially begin. *Dynamo!* Sally said she heard that word in the message and it must have had to do with this. Churchill says if they all join together, they'll be able to bring their boys safely home.

"Do they mean little boats like the *Margaret*?" Aidan asks.

"I think so. The announcer said all the boats."

"But how many boys could the *Margaret* carry?" asks Aidan.

"Didn't he say something about little boats being used as ferries? The smaller boats could bring the soldiers to the bigger ships. Then the bigger ships can go across the Channel."

"Sally, do you think . . . I mean, it sounds so scary and all . . . but do you think the *Margaret* could be part of the rescue effort?"

Sally considers his question. "I don't see why not," she says finally. "They're saying *all* the boats, and the *Margaret*'s a boat, isn't she? So I'd say yes, she certainly can."

"I have to let my dad know!" Aidan says. "He'd be the one to go, of course. I'll tell him."

"Good plan. I'll come with you." She stops for a second though. "Aidan, it's scary to think of going across the Channel, isn't it? I mean, your dad . . . he'd be going right into a war zone."

"Dad's very brave," Aidan says loyally. But the thought frightens him too. "Come on. No time to waste, is there?"

So they hurry down the stairs and back along the pebble-strewn path that leads away from the lighthouse. By the time they reach Aidan's cottage, they are both a little bit out of breath.

"Mum! Dad!" Aidan cries as he bursts through the door. "You'll never guess what we just heard on the radio!"

"Is it about the evacuation and the call for local

boats?" asks Aidan's father. "Operation Dynamo, I believe they're calling it."

"Yes, but how did you know?"

"Your mum and I heard it too. It's quite an undertaking."

Aidan stares at him, confused. Why isn't his dad heading down to the dock to get *Margaret* ready? Instead, Dad's still wearing his slippers and shaking out the newspaper the way he does when he's ready to settle in with it. "Aren't you getting dressed?" Aidan asks. Then he has another thought: Maybe his dad is *scared*. This makes Aidan scared too, as he's never known his father to be afraid of anything.

"Why would I be getting dressed at this hour?" His father pulls his reading glasses out of his pocket.

"To head down to the dock, of course!"

"Now, what would I be doing that for?" asks his father.

"To get the *Margaret* ready to cross the Channel, along with all the other boats." Aidan just can't believe how casual his dad sounds about this.

"I'm not going," Aidan's father says.

"What?" Aidan is properly shocked. "Here's something we can actually do and you say you're not going to do it? Why not? Don't you care about the boys? Don't you care about George?" To his own shame, Aidan feels the tears rising in his eyes and he blinks them away quickly.

His father sighs loudly and puts down the paper. "Of course I care about the boys. Every last one of them, and George most of all. But it's a fool's errand, lad. Our little dory isn't going to make a lick of difference," says his father. "She won't be able to carry very many men."

"The man on the radio said all boats were important," Sally says, and Aidan nods his head vigorously.

"It's a brave effort," Aidan's father says. "But just the same, I'm not going."

Aidan's mother walks into the room then. "Mum, you have to talk to him!" Aidan says. "Tell him he's got to go. He's simply got to."

"Got to go where?"

"To take the *Margaret* across the Channel to

Dunkirk!" Why are he and Sally the only ones who seem to care about this?

"Ah yes, we heard about that on the radio," says his mum. "But our wee boat's not going to help. And we can't risk it. If we lose her, how will your dad go out fishing? He'd have no way of making a living and then where would we be? Out on the street and begging for our supper, that's where." She smooths down the front of her dress. "Best to leave this alone."

"But what about George? George is over there. He needs our help."

"There'll be others going," says his mum. "Now, no more talk of this, do you hear?"

Aidan looks from his father to his mother. They seem calm, and very, very sure of themselves. But he can't believe what they're saying. Not join the others to help the boys? Not be there for George? He's never felt so let down by them in his entire life.

"Maybe we should go outside for a while," whispers Sally. "Come on."

Mutely, Aidan follows her out of the cottage. It's still

light, the waning hours of an ordinary spring day. But it's not ordinary for George or his mates trapped like rats across the sea in France. Once again, stinging hot tears fill Aidan's eyes and he angrily wipes them away. He has to make his mum and dad see the importance of pitching in.

"Maybe your dad could talk to them," says Aidan. "He could change their minds." Sally's family doesn't have a boat, but as the lighthouse keeper, her father holds a special place in their community of sailors and fishermen. "Let's go and ask him. Right now."

They go to Sally's cottage, where her mother is spooning out baked haddock onto a platter. "Sally, Aidan—just in time for supper," she says. "Go wash your hands and come to the table."

Once the food is served, Sally brings up the radio broadcast.

"Oh yes, we heard about that. What a fine thing to do." Sally's dad takes a big forkful of haddock.

"Dad, don't you think Aidan's father ought to take part? After all, he's got a boat."

"He does at that . . ." He chews thoughtfully. "But every man needs to decide that for himself," he adds. "No one can tell him what to do."

"He won't listen to us. But maybe he'll listen to you," Aidan says.

"Maybe," says Sally's father. "Maybe not."

"So you'll talk to him?" Sally asks. "There are so many of our boys at the front, Dad. Not just George. Duncan Campbell, Bobbie Byrne, Will Shepherd . . ." She ticks them off on her fingers.

"I know, but as I said, every man's got to look into his own heart and figure out what's the right thing."

Aidan says nothing. To him, the right thing to do is pretty obvious. Even allowing for his fear—and for his dad's—the answer's still clear.

He eats his haddock quickly and excuses himself before Sally's mum serves the pudding. He has to go back to the cottage to talk to his dad. The boats are already getting ready to leave for Dunkirk. And the *Margaret* just has to go with them.

FOUR

Aidan jogs the whole way home. He finds his dad sitting in his favorite armchair, reading the paper. His mum is darning socks, her needle moving in and out to mend the holes in toes and heels.

"Dad, we just have to join up with the others," Aidan says. "The boys need our help."

"We've already talked about it," his father says. "And the answer is still no: We're not going."

"Leave it be," Mum says.

But Aidan can't leave it. "If you won't go, I'll go by myself," he says. He's bluffing though. Aidan doesn't really want to go by himself. In fact, the mere thought is terrifying, especially after getting the news about Trevor. He's been out on his father's boat scores of times, but he's always stayed close to home, and in waters that are familiar. Crossing the Channel by himself in that little boat would be another thing entirely. He'd be mad to even attempt it.

Dad turns on the radio—music, not news. And when Mum finishes the sock she's working on, she steps next door to visit with Mrs. Pringle.

Aidan feels restless. It's Saturday night and, since there's no school the next day, way too early for bed. He doesn't want to listen to the radio with his dad and he certainly doesn't want to join Mum visiting Mrs. Pringle, who is a nice enough lady but who does go on endlessly about her stomach ailments and her arthritis.

He goes to the door. Maybe he'll join his mum over at Mrs. Pringle's after all. But just as he's about to leave, he sees a tiny bit of blue sticking out from under the doormat. When he pulls out the thin, blue envelope, he recognizes it immediately as a letter from George. Aidan's heart starts a heavy thumping in his chest. The letter hasn't been opened, so clearly Mum and Dad haven't seen it yet. It must have gotten pushed under the mat when the postman dropped the rest of the mail through the slot earlier in the day.

What to do? He should show it to his parents of course. But would it be wrong to open it and read it first? It's addressed to the whole family after all. Mum is still over at Mrs. Pringle's and the radio's still on. Aidan makes a split-second decision and darts up the stairs with the letter. It's only when he's alone in his room with the door closed that he carefully opens it and begins to read.

Dear Mum, Dad, and Aidan,

Not sure how long it will take you to get this letter or where I'll be when you receive it—your last letter took a full month to reach me.

I'd thought that being far from Paris and London would be a good thing, that we'd be safer where we are. But we're getting squeezed harder and harder, even way out here, and we're on the march—it feels to me sometimes like we're on the run. We stop somewhere and then before you turn

around, we pack up and keep going. Pretty soon
we'll reach the coast and then what? No one knows
for sure. The only thing certain here is the uncer-
tainty we face, day by day or even hour by hour.

Anyway, I wish had something more cheering
to report. What I wouldn't give, Mum, for one of
your pre-rationing scones, flaky with butter and
dripping with clotted cream and jam. But that will
have to wait until we've done our job and beaten
Jerry back once and for all.

Think of us. Pray for us. And know that I am
thinking of and praying for you all the time.

Love always,

George

Aidan feels a thundering in his head as he reads these words once, twice, and a third time. *The coast . . . George's unit is heading for the coast.* Dunkirk is on the coast, isn't it? And Dunkirk is where the Germans are headed too—that's why they were talking about it in that message he and Sally were able to intercept. It's bad enough to think that the Germans are threatening any of their boys. But to think that they are threatening George—the realization hits Aidan like a slap to the face. If George does end up in Dunkirk, he'll be trapped and at the mercy of the Germans, and the German soldiers are not known for their mercy. All the while he, Aidan, will be sitting here, doing absolutely nothing to help.

He thinks of what he said to his father: *I'll go myself.* All of a sudden, he means it. Because after reading this letter, despite his fear of the water and his reluctance to disobey his parents, he knows he *has* to go. Maybe his father will relent, and he'll be the one to take the boat across the Channel; Aidan wouldn't be as frightened if he were with Dad. But right now, Dad doesn't want to go, leaving Aidan with little choice. If he wants to join in, he'll just have to go himself.

Aidan tucks the letter in his pocket. He'll show it to his parents later. Right now, he needs to get out of the cottage. Clear his head and all that.

The evening is cool, with no clouds in view, and since the sun hasn't fully set, there's still a glow of pink along the horizon. Aidan ambles down the road and toward the center of town. He passes the sweet shop, the pharmacy, and the post office, all closed for the night.

Then he comes to Dinty's, the pub where his dad likes to go for a pint of ale. The door is open and the place is crowded—men, women, and even some children. Children at a pub? Why is it so packed? Aidan moves closer, until he can hear the voices coming from inside.

". . . and that's why I think we shouldn't be forced to go," someone is saying. Aidan peeps into the open doorway and sees Mr. McAllister, who owns and runs the general store. "We've lost too much already. Much too much." Mr. McAllister's twin boys, Barney and Peter, were both killed a few months ago.

"But if we don't go, the Germans will slaughter more of our boys. We need to rescue them." That's the voice of Mr. Carr, the pharmacist in the village.

"It's too much to ask," Mr. McAllister says. "The risk is too great." *That's what my dad says,* Aidan thinks. But he doesn't speak up. Instead, he slips inside and finds a place on a bench. Clearly he's stumbled on a town meeting. Everyone here is wrestling with the same sort of questions that his dad and mum are wrestling with now. He wants to hear what they have to say.

"May I have the floor?" says Mrs. McAllister. She's a pale, soft-spoken woman, yet she possesses a quiet dignity and composure that make everyone quiet down. They all lean forward to listen to her.

"Ever since we lost Peter and Barney, I've felt like my heart's been cut out of me. I cry every morning, and every night too. But I also know I'm not alone in my grief. So many of you here have felt it too, haven't you?"

A murmur goes around the room, and Aidan sees several people nodding, and one or two wiping their eyes.

"Well, we can't let this go on and on, now can we? Painful as it is, we have to be brave and do our best to rescue the rest of the boys. My own heart may be broken, but it will do me some good to think I can save another mother from the same fate. Churchill's asked for our help and we can't say no to him, can we? Some of the boats are on their way right now. And I'm going to be on our boat, the *Moonlight Sonata*, first thing tomorrow morning. I hope all of you will be there to join me."

There is silence, and then a few people begin to clap, until the whole pub is clapping thunderously and many people rise to their feet. Mr. McAllister is weeping openly. As he embraces his wife, he raises his hand for silence.

"She's the most courageous of all, my Tess," he says. "She's even changed my mind. I can be a stubborn old goat, but I can also admit when I've made a mistake. I'm going to be with her tomorrow. Please join us."

"Amen," calls out someone behind Aidan. And someone lifts a glass in a toast. "To the little ships! And to England—long may she wave!"

Aidan gets up and heads out of the pub. He takes his time walking home because he needs to think. George's letter is burning a hole in his pocket, and his head is abuzz with everything he's seen and heard.

Entering the front room, Aidan finds the radio's been switched off. Dad's settled in his armchair with one of those murder mysteries he favors. Mum's across from him in her rocker, working on the word jumble in the paper.

"Where've you been?" asks Dad.

"Down at Dinty's," Aidan says truthfully.

"Dinty's? The pub's hardly a place for a lad your age." Mum's pencil is suspended midair and she's frowning at him.

"There was something special going on," Aidan says. "A town meeting."

"A town meeting? I didn't hear anything about it," Dad says.

"Mrs. McAllister spoke. She's very brave."

"That poor woman," says Mum. "Not one boy gone, but two."

"That's exactly why we're not going," says Dad. "Enough's enough."

Aidan decides it's time. "A letter came," he says. "It's from George."

"From George!" says Mum. "Let me have it!" As soon as Aidan hands it to her, she begins to read. "So they're heading for the coast." Mum looks up from the letter.

"They could end up stranded there," Aidan points out. "And if we go to meet him, there's a chance we could bring him back. That's what they're talking about, isn't it? Rescuing the boys and bringing them all back home?"

"Not that," his father says. "Not again."

"But, Mum, Dad, don't you see? We have to go! What if George does end up at Dunkirk and we miss the chance to help him because we're not there?"

"We're not going." Dad's gotten all red in the face and his voice is very loud. "Do you hear me? Not going! It's a suicide mission and we're not going to be on it."

"Yes, we are," says Aidan. He turns to his father. "You always taught me to stand up for myself and do what I think is right. Well, that's what I'm going to do. George is out there, Dad. We have to help him."

"I've already lost one boy to this terrible war!" his father thunders. "How much can a man be expected to sacrifice?"

Aidan is shocked. He's never heard his dad lose control like this—never. The naked emotion on his face causes Aidan to look away. But when his gaze turns to his mum, it's even worse. Her face is buried in her hands and she's sobbing.

"Mum . . ." Aidan walks over and touches her shoulder gently.

She raises her face to look at him. "Not another word about this," she says in a fierce and terrible voice. "Not one more word."

"But I thought—"

"Go to your room, young man," she says. "At once."

Aidan doesn't move.

"You heard your mother," says his dad. "Upstairs. Now."

Aidan trudges upstairs, goes into his room, and flops down on the bed. Frustration, anger, confusion are swirling around inside him, a terrible storm of emotions. He's furious that his parents are being so stubborn, but he also feels ravaged by the naked exposure of their grief. Then he hears a light tapping—it sounds like someone is throwing pebbles against the window—and he walks over to investigate. Sally is outside, waving her arms.

Aidan opens the window wide. "What are you doing here?" he calls softly, hoping his parents won't hear.

"I followed you, but when I heard all the commotion inside I thought it was better to wait outside the cottage."

"My dad won't join the others."

"I heard," says Sally. "What are you going to do?"

"I don't know." He looks at Sally. "Stay there," he says. "It'll be easier to talk if I come down and—"

He stops, alerted by an unfamiliar *click*. Has someone locked him in his room? What in the world is going on here?

"Dad?" he calls, rattling the knob. "Mum? Are you out there?"

"Aidan, I'm very sorry to have to do this but Mum and I feel it's the only way."

"Only way for what?" Aidan is confused. "What are you talking about?"

"We have to keep you safe," his mum says. "We've already lost one son to this war. And who knows what could happen to George. You're all we have left and we just can't let you go."

Aidan tries the door again. No luck. He's been jailed, right in his own home! "You've locked me in here?" he asks in disbelief. "Like I'm a prisoner?"

"Not like a prisoner," says Dad. "We're doing it for your own good."

"Dad! Mum!" Aidan pounds on the door with his fists.

"We'll see you tomorrow," says his mum.

Tomorrow! By then, most of the boats will have already left for Dunkirk, to start the hard work of bringing the boys back. Not the *Margaret* though. No, the *Margaret* will be stuck here, idle and useless, all because Aidan's locked up tight. He sinks down to the floor and buries his head in his hands. He's never been so miserable in his whole life.

Suddenly, he jerks his head up. *Sally!*

FIVE

Aidan rushes to the window. Sally is still there. "They've gone and locked me in!" he hisses.

"Oh no!"

"Oh yes!"

"Hello, is anybody there?" calls Aidan's mother. She must have gone downstairs, because she's stepped outside the cottage just as Sally dives down behind a bush.

Silence.

Aidan waits tensely until his mother goes back inside. Sally can't let his parents see her. If she does, they'll send her home. Where is she anyway? The coast is clear now. He waits because he has no other choice. But inside, he's churning, like the sea when it's angry and—

Something shoots past him, sailing in through the open window. He kneels down to retrieve it. It's a paper airplane. He smiles—he and Sally have spent hours folding and refolding planes until they can fly them where they want them to land. When he unfolds this one, he finds a message inside.

I'm going to get a rope so you can slide down. I'll
be right back!

Aidan walks back over to the window. Sure enough, Sally has reappeared, and she's carrying a long, thick coil of rope. She's tied one end around something and he peers outside so he can see what it is—a metal hook. She must have taken it from the lighthouse. But why?

He watches intently while she picks it up and prepares to hurl it. Reaching it high overhead, she lobs the hook toward the window. It goes flying through the air but misses the window and falls down into the shrubbery below.

It makes enough of a noise to attract his mother's attention, and he hears her call out again, "Anybody there?" Aidan's heart is hammering. If his mother goes outside and looks in the bushes, she'll find Sally, and there goes his plan of escape.

But minutes pass and there is no more activity below. Aidan's heart slows. Then he can make out Sally's form again.

Once more, she positions herself on the ground below. Then she throws the hook toward the window, which Aidan has now opened as wide as it will go. This time, it works! The hook clatters to the floor and he is able to use it to pull the rope up and into his room. Now he must secure the rope to something so he can shimmy down. But what?

His glance darts around the familiar space. Bed, desk, bureau—they are all too light to withstand his weight. What about the oak armoire in the corner though? It's very heavy and it rests on a pair of thick, sturdy feet. Yes, the armoire's the thing. He unfastens the hook and loops the end of the rope around the armoire's foot, winding it three times before securely tying it in a clove hitch. Then he sends the rope out the window and down the side of the house. He hopes his parents are in the room on the other side of the cottage so they won't see him coming down.

Carefully, he hoists one leg over the windowsill, grabs on to the rope, and then swings the other leg over too. Sally is waiting below, looking up anxiously at him as he cautiously begins his descent. He lowers himself slowly. *Steady,* he tells himself. *Slow and steady. Almost there.*

As he nears the ground, he can feel a change in the rope's tension. Maybe the weight of his body has dragged the armoire across the floor? Just a little more and then he'll be down and—

He lets go of the rope and falls the last few feet. "Oof!"

Sally rushes over. "Are you all right?" she asks.

Aidan gets up. He's a little wobbly, but unharmed. "Fine," he says. "Only, now that I'm down here, I don't have the faintest idea about what to do." He gives her a searching look. "Do you?"

"You could take the boat out yourself," Sally ventures.

"I don't know if I can do it . . ."

"Of course you can." Sally seems so sure. "You've been going out in that boat for years. You know all about how to handle it."

It's true. He *has* been going out in the *Margaret* for as long as he can remember, and he knows how to set an anchor and coil a rope. He also knows about the tides and currents, and how to read a map. He even knows to steer clear of Goodwin Sands, the ten-mile sandbank in the middle of the Channel that's responsible for so many shipwrecks. But he's never done any of these things by himself. And he's never crossed the whole English Channel and gone all the way to France, even with his dad.

". . . and if we're together, it won't be nearly as scary," Sally is saying.

"Together?" he asks.

"Well, of course! Do you expect me to stay here while you go?"

"Oh. I guess not," Aidan says. The thought of Sally at his side kindles his courage, and he feels much better about the idea of sailing to France.

"So what do you say?" she asks.

"I say we'd better get out of here now, before my mum and dad realize I'm gone!"

Taking the back streets and alleys so they won't be seen, Aidan and Sally hurry along until they are some distance from Aidan's cottage. Then they stop.

"We can't leave now—it's too dark," he points out.

"You're right," says Sally. "We can go at dawn. It'll be safer that way."

"So I'll need a place to spend the night," Aidan says. "I just hope my mum doesn't decide to check on me again."

"Good idea," says Sally. "Now, about tonight . . ."

In the end, they go back to Sally's cottage. Aidan hides in the woodshed while Sally manages to slip inside her house. She comes back with a down comforter, a blanket, and a pillow. Then she helps Aidan make a bed in the shed.

"Will you be all right out here?"

"I'll be fine."

"Good night, then," she says. "See you in the morning."

"Good night." Aidan settles down in his makeshift

bed. It's not so bad out here. He hears a hooting sound—a barn owl most likely—and then a scurrying sound in the grass nearby. A predator is hunting and its prey is scrambling for safety. *Like George,* he thinks. Only he's going to help George, not leave him to fend for himself in his hour of need.

Aidan is too keyed up to fall asleep right away and when he does, the dream comes again. This time, the monstrous wave is bigger, darker, and more menacing than ever before, and when he wakes, he's sweating even though the night is cool. Too bad Maude's not here to *purr* him back to sleep. Eventually, he dozes off again, and then before he knows it, it's dawn and Sally's shaking him awake.

"Come on, we should go," she says, handing him a heel of bread she's pulled from her pocket. "It's a bit stale but there wasn't anything else," she says.

Aidan munches on it as they make their way down to the dock, hoping not to be stopped along the way. When they get there, they see a scant few of their neighbors getting into their own boats. Aidan thinks again of Mrs. McAllister's moving words and the rousing response she received. He doesn't see the *Moonlight Sonata* but he's sure that's because it's already on its way. What about the others though? Have they all forgotten what they heard and promised last night? But it doesn't matter because there's no time to be thinking about all this now. He and Sally are on an urgent mission and they have to hurry.

Once they're aboard the *Margaret*, the first thing they do is haul the wet nets and all the fishing tackle off the boat. They'll need every inch of room for the men they are going to transport. Sally pulls up the anchor while Aidan turns on the engine, and eases away from the dock. He hopes there'll be enough fuel to see them there and back—they were in such a rush that he forgot to stop and get an extra can. But his dad always keeps a spare can stowed away. They can use that if they have to.

When the engine is humming, Aidan consults the map, just to double-check the route. His heart is still hammering and he wants to calm down so he can think straight—he'll need all his wits about him.

Suddenly, he hears his name being called. "Aidan!" He turns to see his parents running down the dock, waving their arms frantically. His father's hair is sticking out wildly from his head, and his mother still wears her nightdress with a raincoat thrown over it. "Come back!" yells his father.

"You'll be killed!" his mother cries.

Aidan is stabbed by guilt when he sees their stricken faces. But he can't let that change his mind or let himself think of the worst that could happen. He has to forge ahead. "I've got to be brave. We all do." *I'm doing this for George,* he thinks. *George is somewhere out there, and he needs our help.* Aidan turns away.

Sally looks at him for a moment. "You all right?" she asks.

"I think so," he says. "There's nothing they can do from the dock anyway."

The voices of his parents grow fainter and fainter until he can't hear them at all. He looks out over the choppy water. Although Operation Dynamo has already begun, Aidan prays they can still catch up with the flotilla of boats making their way across the Channel—if they hurry. But the water is rough and it won't be easy. Still, they've gotten this far and there's no way he's going to back down now.

"How long do you think it will take to cross the Channel?" Sally asks.

"I've never actually done it," he says. "But I'm guessing between two and three hours, depending on the tide and the wind. We'll just follow the others and we should be all right."

"Look at that." Sally points toward another vessel, a pleasure boat from the sleek look of her. The man on board is hoisting a Union Jack on a pole; the flag snaps and flutters in the stiff breeze.

"I think we've got a flag on board somewhere," he says to Sally. "Want to see if you can find it?"

Sally rummages around and comes up with a small, rather wrinkled flag. "It's better than nothing," she says.

Aidan watches her attach the familiar flag to the railing of the *Margaret*. He feels a swell of pride. "No," he says, "it's not just better than nothing. It's absolutely grand."

Far away, across the Channel in France, George and his mates are on their way to Dunkirk. Some of the men say they're going to meet a hospital ship, and the idea of that ship is like a shining mirage in George's mind: It promises sleep and a hot meal. George has had about two hours of sleep in the last twenty-four and is hungry enough to eat the sole of his combat boot, so he cannot wait to get there.

The men started off on foot but they were picked up by a group of trucks, and as they rattle along the dirt road in the convoy, George keeps his eyes on the sky. German planes circle ominously above, targeting hamlets to be dive-bombed later. But the planes above leave them alone—at least for now.

They drive up one lane, down the next, along rutted

old cart tracks—anywhere but on the main roads, where bomb craters gape open like hideous mouths. The side roads are clogged with troops and other convoys and it's slow going. And then the vehicle stops altogether.

"What's going on?" calls out the corporal.

"It's an ambulance," comes the reply. "Ran into a ditch."

George cranes his neck out the window to look. Sure enough, there's the ambulance, blocking the road ahead. He hears patients calling out for water, and others wailing in pain.

Meanwhile, Jerry is dropping their parachute flares all over the countryside. They begin as little bursts of light, but as they come down, they grow larger and more menacing. By the time they land, they are full-blown fires, devastating whatever they touch.

George grows more and more anxious. Ignoring strict instructions against it, the driver is flashing his lights, and George is sure Jerry will spot their vehicles. But all he can do is wait here with the others. Finally, the ambulance is dragged aside and the trucks start up again.

Overcome by fatigue, George closes his weary eyes. *Just a few minutes,* he thinks. *Just a few . . .*

Suddenly, there's a loud noise—some kind of explosion. George's eyes fly open and his arms reflexively shoot out, so that he hits Neville, who is sitting next to him on the convoy.

"Watch it," Neville grumbles.

"Sorry, mate," he says.

They've come to the town and are speeding along a road that runs parallel to the canal. The sky is brilliant with shell bursts, and gunfire explodes all around them.

"Hey, I thought we were headed to a safe haven," Neville says, his irritation instantly forgotten.

George stares at the dense gray cloud hanging low over the town, the furiously churning sea, and the smoke from the huge oil storage drums—they must have just been bombed. This is no haven. This is his worst nightmare.

* * *

The wind is picking up. The *Margaret*'s engine is old and not all that powerful, and it seems to Aidan as if they are staying in place instead of making any forward progress. Despite the brisk sea air, he's warm and even sweating. He thinks of his brother and of the hundreds of other boys, stranded and in urgent need of their help. If he and Sally are ever going to reach them, they have to go faster. He strains to see ahead of them, hoping to catch sight of anything that means they're nearly there, and—look, there in the far distance is one of the boats from the flotilla! It's tiny but the sight propels him. He's going to reach it, he knows he can—

Kaboom!

Suddenly, a streak of what seems like fire shoots down toward the water, landing in a shower of fiery sparks just a few meters from the dory. Although the dory wasn't hit, the water around it churns violently and the little boat shudders from the impact.

"What in the world—" cries Sally.

Before Aidan can answer, there is another loud blast from the sky. This one explodes in an angry shower of red sparks right in front of the dory. An acrid, burning smell fills Aidan's nostrils, but even worse are the coils of gray, dense smoke that plume overhead. Aidan begins to cough and he hears Sally coughing too. His eyes water and he swipes at them furiously.

As the smoke begins to drift away, Aidan cautiously looks up. To his horror, he sees a plane positioned virtually right above them! Those missiles or bombs or whatever are coming from that plane—it must be part of the German Luftwaffe.

"Sally . . ." he croaks. "Sally, can you see what's up there?"

"See it? It's practically on top of us!" She's right; the German plane is directly overhead now. "We'd better duck or we're going to get slammed!"

George and his unit start across the wide, flat beach with its hard-packed sand. Behind them are a hotel, a café, and a restaurant, all shut up tight as drums. Ahead lies the ocean, where he can see downed planes and the wreckage of sunken ships, ominous reminders of the enemy's brutal strength. In between are the hordes of men, pushed to water's edge and waiting for rescue. When, how, and if it will come is anyone's guess.

The noise is deafening. Frantic and in search of cover, George scrambles toward a pile of sandbags and crouches down behind them, his eyes nervously darting here and there, trying to take in the whole scene. The chaos he saw from the window of the convoy is nothing compared to what is happening now. Jerry is blitzing Dunkirk in a full-scale attack. Along the canal bank, soldiers are shuffling and stumbling toward the docks. They are filthy and worn-out, many just limping along. With mounting terror, George realizes that they aren't withdrawing in a strategic way. They are fleeing a brutal enemy that is coming at them from all sides.

A senior officer strides up and stops the mass of soldiers from advancing. George gets up from his hiding place and hurries to join them; he wants to hear the officer, who is now barking orders.

"...you're being sent to a quay farther down the beach, one convoy at a time, in three-minute intervals," he says. "You'll be given air protection when you get there."

George and the others nervously await their turn. Sand is everywhere—in his shoes, under his uniform, in his mouth, and in his eyes. The explosions continue, and each one slaps into the ground and makes George's rib cage shake. Finally, the men pile into the third truck in the convoy. George is flung backward as the big vehicle lurches into gear.

He rights himself and peers outside. And gasps. The town, which had seemed quiet but intact just a little while ago, has been destroyed. Roads are pocked with craters and strewn with debris from the bombs—bricks, girders, massive chunks of buildings. George sees a dead horse, and then another. But worse are the dead people—men, women, and even children—lying still where they have fallen.

When they finally reach the quay, George sees that bombs have torn away huge sections of the concrete. The embankment has been blown up in one place, and water is gushing out, flooding the fields. It's a sight as horrifying as it is terrifying—an image of destruction that will make escaping even harder.

The driver turns off the motor and they wait. After about twenty minutes, a formation of planes appears in the sky above. *Thank goodness,* thinks George. *Our flyboys are here—finally.* But relief turns to despair when he realizes, no, those aren't English planes, not at all. They're German planes, and they are swooping down, intent on destroying everyone and everything below. *Where are our boys? Why has the RAF abandoned us to be slaughtered on these beaches, covered in sand, sweat, and raw terror?*

There is a stampede for shelter as the men, not willing to be sitting ducks, fight and push their way out of the truck. But there are only two remaining sandbagged dugouts on the quay and they can't hold very many men. There's no room for George, so he runs across the wooden planks over the dugout and jumps onto the deck of a barge. He twists his ankle in the fall but barely registers the pain.

Bullets and shrapnel rain down all around him and the screams of the wounded resound in his head. The land and the sea are shaking with the awful impact of the bombs.

A German soldier jumps onto the barge and suddenly he and George are face-to-face, eyeing each other warily. The German's face is slick and black with oil—he must have landed in the water after his plane exploded.

George sees Jerry position his machine gun and take aim but some superhuman force comes over George. He tackles the German before he can fire. There is a fierce, brief scuffle, all fists, knees, and sharp elbows. At first it seems like the German is winning as he pins George down with his powerful arms. But George's legs are free and he uses both of them to deliver a fierce kick that knocks the German soldier right off of him and onto the deck. George charges, using his shoulder as a battering ram, and pushes him over the railing and off of the barge. The German lands with a loud splash. Beyond the railing, George can see the man flailing frantically in the waves. He must have inhaled a lot of water, because he is coughing, sputtering, and trying desperately to stay afloat. But the heavy ammunition strapped to his chest drags him down, deep below the surface. In a matter of moments, the German is swallowed up and gone, claimed forever by the sea.

George is stunned. He didn't shoot the man, but he was responsible for his death just the same, and the knowledge is a shock to his soul. He knows he had no choice. If he hadn't pushed him, the German would have killed him on the spot. That's what war is—kill or be killed. And yet the German soldier was a person, not just a faceless enemy. He was a young man, probably a lot like George himself, or the soldier from the barn, whose wallet is still in George's pack. But this is no time for pondering such weighty moral and ethical questions. This barge isn't safe and George has to get out of here—immediately.

* * *

Aidan crouches, arms over his head, as the missiles rain down all around them. The sound is deafening and the explosives fill the air with smoke. Aidan's throat and lungs begin to burn. Coughing and gasping, he frantically digs in his pocket. It must be here, it *has* to be here—there it is! With trembling fingers, he dips the wadded-up handkerchief from his pocket into the pool of water that has collected at the bottom of the boat. Then he places the wet cloth over his mouth and nose— ah, that's *so* much better. His brother George told him about that trick, and it works.

But Sally's breathing is still labored and harsh.

"Do you have a handkerchief?" he says.

"W-why are you asking about a handkerchief now?" She can barely get the words out.

Aidan's mind is racing as fast as his heart. The missiles continue to land, though now they are not so close— maybe all the smoke has made it hard for the pilot to see the position of the boat? But they are still stuck here and if Sally is choking—Aidan looks down at his shirt-tails, which have come untucked from his pants.

He takes a shirttail in his hands and yanks once, twice—no, the material is too strong, but he has to, he *has* to—he pulls again, using all the force he has, and this time he is able to rip off a piece. He could weep with relief.

He dips the torn cloth in the water and hands it to Sally. "Here," he barks. "Put it over your nose." She copies the way he's holding his own handkerchief, and in seconds her breathing eases. And it looks like the plane may have moved on too—there haven't been any new missiles in the last few minutes.

With shaking legs, Aidan stands and offers Sally a hand up. That was a close call, but the worst seems to be over. Now they have to summon the strength and will to keep going. Again, George's words echo in Aidan's mind. *I can be brave, George*, he silently promises his brother. *I can and I will*. But just then, he hears a whistling noise, and he freezes. A final missile comes hurtling down—and this one hits the nose of the little dory straight on.

SIX

George scrambles off the barge, looking for another, safer place to hide. He sees several men in front of the dugout and the sight is chilling. The heavy sandbags have been pushed and the men are lifting bodies Wounded?—from the opening, and carrying them off. Cautiously, George creeps closer. He doesn't know what happened. But when one of the men turns to him and says, "Go on, get in—there's room now," he doesn't ask any questions; he just scrambles inside. It's hot and crowded and the sound of the missiles hurtling down makes everyone jumpy. Every time George hears it he flinches.

After a while, though, the sound of the missiles tapers off—Jerry must be off bombing elsewhere—and the men begin to relax just a little. Someone produces a sack of apples and starts passing the fruit around. George takes his apple, and though it's bruised and mealy, he's grateful for the sweetness it offers. It's gone in minutes and when he's passed another—this one mostly rotted—he eats that one too. Nothing like his mum's apple tarts, of course . . . or even the cinnamon-laced applesauce she liked to serve with a pork roast. Then the men start to talk, and he can feel an almost electrical current buzzing through the chatter.

On the beach, they said . . . boats are coming . . . rescue operation . . . Dynamo, they're calling it. Operation Dynamo.

So the British navy is conducting a rescue operation? But with what boats? How are they going to rescue anyone? He looks around and bolts upright when he sees that some of the men are making their way outside again. "Where are they going?" he asks.

"Down to the water, mate," says the fellow standing next to him. "The little ships are coming to take us home."

George follows him from the dugout. Even in the darkness, the scene is still horrifying to behold, and for a few seconds George wants to go right back inside, away from the destroyed buildings, knee-deep rubble, and everywhere the awful stench of burnt buildings and garbage. He thinks he will be sick right on the spot, but he takes a few deep breaths and keeps going, marching along with the others and finally running down to the water. When he reaches the shore, he can see dozens, scores, maybe even hundreds of men milling around.

And then he sees the lights on the boats, tiny as toys at first, but growing bigger by the minute. Can this really be true—that this motley, ragtag little armada is coming here, to Dunkirk, to gather them up and take them home? It just doesn't seem possible. But look— they're here!

It's amazing that the dory hasn't been smashed to bits. But it's been badly damaged and water is seeping in at an alarming rate. Aidan and Sally are bailing out as fast as they can. Still, their efforts are not enough: They have to figure out a way to repair the boat.

"What are we going to do?" Sally says. Her hair is plastered to her face and forehead, and she pushes it back out of her eyes.

"Can you handle the bailing while I go find the tool kit?"

"Yes," she says. "But hurry!"

The tool kit is always kept in a cupboard right up front, but when Aidan opens the door, it's not there. Panic rises up like the waves hitting the boat. Where could it be? He gropes around on the shelf. Finally, his hand clasps the familiar wooden box and he's flooded with relief.

He pulls the box onto his lap and opens it up. Wrench, hammer, nails, and a saw, but nothing that can help him now. He looks around the boat frantically. What about those life vests? Can they be stuffed into the opening and sealed up with—well, exactly what isn't clear at the moment but there's no time to think it through—he's got to try something. He tosses one of the vests to Sally. "Can you stuff that in there?" he asks.

"Umm, let's see," she says. It takes her a few minutes to position it and wedge it in tightly, and she holds it in place as she swivels to look at Aidan. "Do you have another?" she asks.

He grabs the others and tosses them over one at a time. To his amazement and relief, the flow of water is stopped by the four life vests that have been crammed into the opening. But Aidan is pretty sure that once the boat picks up speed, their makeshift repair won't be watertight. They have to figure out some way to seal the crevices around the life vests.

"Maybe we can use the flag," says Sally. She detaches it from the boat and crams it into the hole. "And that tarp too."

The tarp was folded up and Aidan hadn't even noticed it. "We'll fit it around the life vests and secure it somehow."

"Good idea," Aidan says, and immediately gets to it. The tarp is kind of bulky and flaps in the wind but Aidan manages to subdue it enough to wrap around the mass of life jackets. It looks like a mess but who cares? At least the water's not seeping in any longer. Meanwhile, Sally is rummaging around in the tool kit. She finds a roll of steel wool and several sponges and reaches under the tarp to stuff all of it underneath. Now the section of tarp covering the life jackets is pulled taut. "There," she says, stepping back. "I think it looks pretty seaworthy."

"Good work," says Aidan. "We should keep going." He consults the compass and adjusts the dials. They sail on, battered but undefeated. Soon they start to see ships, just a few at first, then more and more as they press ahead. There are tugboats and sailboats, pleasure boats and fishing boats—even a rowboat or two. The bigger boats and the tugboats pull the smaller boats in their wake—that must be their way of conserving fuel.

Even as Aidan thinks this, the *Margaret*'s engine begins to sputter. *Oh no*. Aidan knows all too well what this means—they're out of petrol.

"What's wrong?" asks Sally. "The engine sounds funny."

"We're out of petrol," he tells her. "Let me just get the extra can." The boat's not moving now, so Aidan gets up to search for the petrol. He finds the can, tucked away where it always is. The only trouble is that it's light as a wicker basket—there's nothing in it. Like the empty bait bucket, the empty petrol can is one more sign that his dad isn't minding the boat properly. Aidan brings the empty can to show Sally.

"What are we going to do?" she says. Aidan hears the fear in her voice.

"I don't know." He can see other boats out on the water, but none of them are in shouting distance. And even though Sally's a good swimmer—he's teased her by saying she was born underwater, and with fins—it's just too far between boats in this cold, choppy ocean for her to attempt safely.

Anxiously, Aidan scans the horizon, praying that a solution will come to him. And it does. In the distance, he can make out the lines of a rowboat, painted white, and it reminds him that there is a pair of oars tucked into a special compartment under the seat. His father keeps them there for emergencies—or at least he did. Who knows if they're still there, or what condition he'll find them in?

Quickly, he opens the compartment and is bathed with relief. The oars are still there. They look a little dried out, but they'll do the job. "Here." He hands an oar to Sally. "Can you row?" Aidan takes the other oar and then he and Sally position themselves on either side of the boat. "All right," Aidan says. "Let's go!"

The current is against them and Aidan feels like they are rowing through sludge, not water, as they struggle and strain to push the oars through the waves. It's hard work, and rowing is a treacherous business— it's so easy to get thrown off course. But he tries to use the boats in the distance as a guide.

For the longest time, it seems as if they are not moving at all, but rowing in place. Aidan's hands are slippery with sweat, and his arms are aching too. He can feel a blister forming in the place between his thumb and forefinger. It hurts. But he cannot stop rowing.

"Do you think we're getting anywhere?" Sally asks.

"Yes." He's quiet for a moment. "No. I really can't tell. Can you?"

"No." She lets the oar rest for a moment to wipe her brow. Then she picks it up and they begin again. The wind has changed though, and now it feels like they *are* moving, slowly at first, and then a little faster.

At last, the lights of the other ships look closer, and closer still. And then it seems as if they are surrounded by them, the brightness of the lanterns reflecting on the dark water. Each of these boats is going to Dunkirk. And so is the *Margaret*.

Aidan's heart fills with pride as he looks at all these brave men and women, defying the odds and rushing to help their boys in danger. And he's even more proud that he and Sally are a part this courageous effort. He stretches out his arm and waves to some of the people whose forms he can make out in the dark.

"Ahoy!" cries an old man who wears a black woolen cap. The stout woman at his side returns his wave, moving her arm in a swooping, graceful motion.

George spots CO Rogers and rushes over. He's been separated from his unit ever since they arrived in Dunkirk and he's relieved to find him again.

"You're all right, then?" asks Rogers.

"Aye, sir," says George.

There's a pause, and Rogers says, "Then you and I are the only ones who are."

"What are you talking about?" asks George.

"We took a hit," says Rogers. "Just as we debussed. We lost five men instantly. And everyone else is wounded."

"Who did we lose?" George asks. But does he really want to know?

"Chambers, Ivers, Crowson, Dillard, and Westin." Rogers rattles off the names.

George can picture each of them so clearly in his mind. Now they are gone—all gone. "And the rest of the men, sir?" He wills his voice not to crack.

"Taken to the emergency medical vehicle. Docs

will patch them up as best they can—supplies are low and some of those men were in pretty bad shape when they went in." Rogers gives George a shrewd and appraising look. "It's just you and me, mate," he says with a sigh. "We're the only ones from our unit left and now it's up to us to carry on."

Together, they turn toward the sea. The boats are coming closer now. "Let's start with getting our lads aboard," says the CO.

"Aye, aye, sir." George salutes, turns, and wades into the chilled, churning sea.

SEVEN

It's almost noon, but the sky overhead is gray and overcast. A few gulls circle above, hungry and looking for a meal. The sound of their cries is mournful and jarring.

Even though he and Sally have been up since dawn, Aidan is anything but tired. The events of the last few hours have sharpened all of his senses and his whole body feels tightly wound and on high alert.

Aidan and Sally got fuel from another of the small boats a little while ago, and now they are nearing the beach at Dunkirk. The water is teeming with soldiers. Most are Tommies but he recognizes some French and Belgian uniforms mixed in too. And somewhere in this crowd of anxious, desperate men is his brother. Or at least he hopes he is—for all Aidan knows, George could be wounded somewhere. Or dead. No. He won't let himself think that way. Instead, he forces himself to focus on an image of George as he was on the day he shipped out, uniform neat and pressed, cap set jauntily on his head.

"George is here, on this beach. I can feel it," Aidan says to Sally.

"He has to be," Sally says. "I just hope we find him."

"We'll find him, all right," says Aidan. "I'm sure of it."

Just in front of them are three British soldiers. One is tall and skinny, another is short and skinny, and they are holding the elbows of a third man, who can't seem to stand on his own. The wounded man's eyes are closed and he moans softly in pain.

"We can easily take these three," says Sally. "And maybe even a fourth. See that big boat over there?" She points to a large vessel at some distance out in the water. "We'll bring the men out to it."

"Not yet," says Aidan. "I want to find George before we start helping anyone else."

"But what about these soldiers?"

"We'll help them after. First I've got to find George. He's my brother, after all."

"I know he's your brother." Sally's voice sounds clipped. "But that means we're going to leave these men. How can we do that? They're counting on our help."

As if on cue, the soldier in the middle moans again. His face is deathly pale and Aidan can see beads of sweat on his forehead. How badly is he wounded?

"It's my dad's boat," Aidan says. "I'm in charge here." He doesn't like to bring this up, but Sally's being so stubborn—he has no other choice. "I didn't have to take you along with me."

"No, but you're lucky you did," Sally says quietly. "I fixed that leak, didn't I? We're a team and you should remember it."

"Who says I don't?" Aidan is sullen because he knows she's right and her words shame him slightly. She's thinking not just of them, but of the reason they've come all this way.

Aidan looks at the three men in the water, waves

lapping at their knees. They're shivering. "Can you climb up?" he calls out.

"We sure can," says the tall soldier.

"What about your mate there?" asks Sally. "He looks like he's been hurt."

"We'll pull him up. The two of us can manage it."

Aidan brings the boat in closer and the two men hoist their comrade up and gently place him onto the floor of the boat. Then the two other men climb aboard. The tall one pulls a blanket from his clobber and covers the wounded man, then stuffs the clobber under the man's head for a pillow. Aidan takes off in the direction of the larger boat. As soon as he and Sally reach the larger boat, the men climb out and up the net ropes that have been let down for them. Sally waves but Aidan just watches silently as the bigger boat moves away. He doesn't even know their names, he thinks. And they'll never know his.

Having delivered their passengers safely, Aidan and Sally head back toward the shore. More men are waiting in the water, waving their arms in the air, desperate to be picked up.

Aidan is torn. He wants so badly to find George, but all these men need their help too. Each one is someone's son, husband, brother, best friend. Each one has family and friends, a whole host of people praying for their safety, waiting for him to come home. Aidan can't abandon these men any more than he would be able to abandon George.

For hours, Aidan and Sally work side by side, helping soldiers—some of them wounded, all of them famished and exhausted—to the larger boats as they arrive. Aidan is hungry and thirsty, and at one point, he gratefully accepts a sip of water from the canteen one of the soldiers offers him and Sally. "You look like you could use a hand too," says the soldier. "It's not an easy job you took on here."

Despite his fatigue, Aidan smiles as he hands the canteen back to the soldier. "We're in this thing together," he says. "Back home, we've all been thinking of you. Day and night. And now we have the chance to help."

Bombs continue to explode—clearly Jerry's keeping busy. For now, the explosions are at some distance—Aidan can see the planes though they are still far off in the sky. Who knows how long they'll have this brief reprieve? Aidan and Sally try to step up the pace, keenly aware that the blasts on the horizon may soon be much, much closer. Aidan can only pray that George is all right, and that someone else is helping him, the way he and Sally are helping the men they see. Because that's what this is about it, isn't it? Each of them helping in any way that they can.

After a while, the faces and voices of the men begin to blur. It doesn't matter. Aidan is deep in the rhythm now. Bring the boat in, gather a few men, and ferry them to a larger boat, then turn around and start again. Stop to refuel if necessary. He and Sally do this over and over and over. It begins to seem like they've never done anything else. And that they never will.

* * *

It's tough going, thinks George as he slogs through the water to escort the men into the waiting boats. At first he's surprised to see that there's not a military boat in the batch. They're all manned by civilians, and some of the ships are such wee things that they barely have enough room for two passengers. But every last one of them is important.

The boats have come from up and down the British coast—Dover, Deal, Kent—and George is enormously moved that all these people, folks no different from his mum and dad, have risked so much to travel here this morning. He wonders how his mum and dad are, and makes a vow to write to them as soon as he's able. And he wonders if anyone from his hometown is here in these waters today—it's certainly possible. It's even possible that his parents could be here . . . But enough daydreaming. He's got a job to do. Resolutely, George turns to the soldier who's been leaning heavily on the arm of his friend, waiting patiently until it's their turn.

"He's lost a lot of blood," says the friend. "There weren't any medics, so I decided to take him with me. Just want to get him home is all. Home's the place for him. They'll fix him up as good as new."

"Here," George says. "I'll get on one side and you get on the other, and we'll head toward that fishing boat right there." He gestures farther out. "She'll ferry you both to that tugboat." But when George reaches for the other man's arm to hoist it over his own shoulder, the man lets out a howl of excruciating pain and doubles over, nearly knocking George off-balance and into the water.

"Easy now, mate," says George, hovering near the wounded soldier. He needs to take his arm if he's going to get him into that boat, so very carefully, he tries again. This time, the soldier twists so violently that he's the one knocked off-balance and he lands face-first in the water.

"Hugh!" cries his friend. "Hugh, are you all right?" He drags Hugh to his feet, dries his face with his sleeve, and attempts to prop him up again. But Hugh is not responding and doesn't seem able to stand, even with help. His head is slumped, his eyes are closed, and a thin trickle of blood leaks from the corner of his mouth. His face is an awful, bleached color, like an old sheet.

George puts a hand on Hugh's chest. Nothing. Then he reaches for Hugh's wrist to get a pulse. There is none. "I'm afraid Hugh is . . . gone," he says as gently as he can.

"Gone!" echoes the friend. "What are you talking about? He can't be gone. He was fine just an hour ago, right as rain. Then that cursed grenade exploded. Got him in the side, ripped a hole in him. I didn't want to leave him behind; I thought he'd be better off with me. But I was wrong—it's my fault that he's dead." He buries his face in his hands.

"No, it's not your fault." George tries to comfort the grieving man. "Not unless you started this war." The man keeps his face covered, muffling the sound of his sobs. "Where are you from?" George asks him.

"Devonshire." The man lifts his face and swipes at his red-rimmed eyes.

"Don't you want to go back home and see your folks? Let me help you."

The man allows himself to be led to the boat. But he won't let go of Hugh and drags the heavy, lifeless body behind him and through the water. "I'm bringing him back with me," he says. "His family will want to give him a decent burial."

George nods. Once the man is safely on board, he turns to help the next man, and then the next. There are so many, the line stretching endlessly behind them. He sees them into the small boats and once these boats have brought them to the larger vessels, they come back again, ready to receive more passengers.

But after a couple of hours, it's clear that there is another problem and it's a major one: There are no more big boats, only the little ones.

George slogs through the water and finds his CO on the beach. "No more big boats, sir," he reports.

"I know." Rogers sighs. "Maybe we'll start using the smaller boats to carry 'em across until the big boats came back. Even taking two or three at a time would be better than nothing."

"But there are so many men, sir. We won't be able to save them all."

"No," says Rogers. "We won't." His face looks sad and weary. "We'll do the best we can though, won't we?"

"Aye, sir." George salutes before wading back into the water, ready to help the next soldier. This time it's a group of three men that he escorts, bringing them to a small dory with the name *Margaret* written in script across the prow. What a funny coincidence—that's the name of his dad's boat.

And when he looks up, he realizes that seeing the boat is more than a coincidence—it's a regular miracle, because he's staring straight at his father's boat. And standing at the steering wheel and looking anxiously out at the water is none other than his little brother, Aidan. Aidan! How in the world did he get here?

But before he can even call out his brother's name,

a loud noise from above makes him spin around and look up. There, in the gray-blue sky, are Jerry's planes, flying in strict formation. They've been at some distance for a while, but they're now moving in closer—again.

There are still dozens of men in the water, and not enough boats to get them out of here. What's going to happen now? George can't even begin to imagine. "Aidan!" he shouts, signaling wildly to attract his brother's attention. "Aidan, over here!" But the words are swallowed up, drowned out by the awful roaring of the planes that are overhead and moving right toward them.

EIGHT

Aidan has just started moving toward a soldier in need of transport when a persistent buzzing up above causes him to glance quickly into the sky. There, in a sharp formation, are the German planes that had been off in the distance earlier in the day. Now they are getting closer and their mission is clear.

Aidan turns to Sally, but before he can utter a word, he hears his name being called out, again and again. He whips around, trying to see where the voice is coming from. When his eyes settle on the source of the voice, his mouth falls open in astonishment. It's George! George is here, and he's calling to him!

"Sally, look!" he cries, grabbing her arm and directing her gaze. "George is out there! Do you see him?"

Sally's eyes scan the water and then she sees him too. "We found him!"

"Or he found us!" Aidan immediately steers the boat toward George, just as George is making his way through the water toward the *Margaret*, and when the boat is close enough, Aidan scrambles down and into the water.

George grabs him, and for a few seconds the two brothers embrace tightly, not saying a word. It's only when George releases him that the questions start tumbling out, one after the next.

"How in the world did you get here? Do Dad and Mum know? How are they? How are *you*?"

Aidan doesn't answer right away. He just stands there in the water, grinning. George is alive and standing right in front of him. His brother looks older. Thinner too. His uniform is wrinkled and filthy. But he's here, he's really here. And now Aidan and Sally can bring him back to England.

"Mum and Dad—they do know we're here, but they didn't want me to come. In fact, they flat-out locked me in my room. Sally helped spring me though. And now we're here, which is where we belong."

"Poor Mum . . ." George says. "After Trevor and all, she must be mad with worry."

"I know," says Aidan. "And I'm truly sorry to make her unhappy. But I went to the town meeting and, oh, you should have heard them there, George. Especially Mrs. McAllister. She lost both her boys, you know, but she was so determined that she had the whole town wanting to pitch in and help. And then I got your last letter and I realized I had to come find you. And look— we did."

"You're very brave," says George. Then he looks over at Sally. "You're the bravest two kids in all of England. Maybe even all of Europe."

Sally is grinning at the compliment and Aidan feels so proud that his courageous soldier brother thinks he's been courageous too. But his mission isn't over yet. He's got to get George safely back to England. Then, and only then, will Aidan feel he's done the job he set out to do.

". . . they told us we'd be safe at Dunkirk, that we'd get a hot meal and some rest," George is saying. "But it wasn't like that at all. When we got here, the city was already under siege." He glances up. "And it's about to begin again."

"I know. So hurry up and get in the boat and we can get you out of here as soon as possible. There aren't any more big boats. But we got across the Channel and we'll get back across it again if we hurry." And this time he'll make sure he has a spare can of petrol before they attempt to make the crossing.

"Aidan, I can't leave now," George says.

"What do you mean?"

"Just what I said. My unit took a serious hit. Five men were killed straightaway and everyone else was hurt, some pretty badly. My CO and I are the only ones left standing. We've got to stay here and see this thing through."

"But we've come all this way for you! We want to help you. We can't just leave you here."

"You are helping me," says George. "Seeing you and

Sally has boosted my spirits more than I can even say. But my duty is here and my mind's made up. I couldn't leave now even if I wanted to."

Aidan is crushed. Leave George here, when the German planes are so close—how could he do such a thing? "No. I'm not leaving without you," he says. "I'm going to stay right here until you get into this boat."

George smiles, a weary smile that doesn't touch the sadness Aidan can see in his eyes. "You're a good, loyal brother," he says. "I'm proud of you, I really am. And I want you to be proud of me too. That means I have to obey my orders and stay here." He gestures to the hordes of men waiting on the beach. "Besides, it's not even my turn. How would it look to the others if I went back with you just because we're brothers? Would that be right? Or fair?"

"I suppose not . . ." Aidan says.

"You know it wouldn't. Yes, I'm your brother, but all those boys out there, well, they're our brothers too. We can't let them down, not even a single one."

Aidan looks at George. His expression is so serious and so resolute that Aidan knows there's no arguing.

"Send my love to Mum and Dad," George says. "Tell them I'll write to them as soon as I can. But I've got to be going now. My lieutenant is waiting for me." George reaches out and hugs Aidan again. Aidan wishes he never had to let him go.

When he finally does, he remains in the water, watching as George makes his way toward the beach. When George gets to the shore, he turns and waves. And he smiles. Even from here, Aidan can see it's one of those sad smiles, the kind that isn't about joy as much as it is about endurance. Then George begins to jog in the direction of a jeep where a soldier is waiting behind the wheel.

"Come on, get in!" calls Sally. She's still in the boat and has seen—and heard—everything. Aidan climbs into the boat just as the first flashes start up. The Germans are dropping bombs now. They're still some distance off but the sight and sound of them are terrifying.

"Let's take as many as we can and start heading back," Aidan says. Sally nods. If they squeeze in, they can take four men across. Four hardly seems like very many, though it's better than none.

But before they can pick up any of the men, the planes above begin to drop their terrifying cargo. The skin on the back of Aidan's neck prickles each time he hears the whooshing of a missile falling toward the soldiers in the water. The brilliant streaks of heat and flame shoot down, but some of them don't land on the water; some of them land right on the men waiting for the boats that have come to save them. Aidan can't tear his gaze away as a boat capsizes, spilling its wounded passengers into the waves. A man flies high into the air and then drops, a broken puppet, into the water below.

Aidan closes his eyes. He doesn't want to see any more. But it's useless. The images are already burned into his memory—he can never forget them. And even without seeing what's happening, he can still hear the explosions and the agonized screams of those who've been hit. How he and Sally have not been hit is a miracle, and he knows it will not last. To think they could have come so far and endured so much, only to be crushed now that they've reached their men and are on the way home—

"What's the matter with you?" Sally screams. "We have to get out of here!"

Aidan opens his eyes. There is a lone soldier standing just a few feet away from them in the water. He looks so young—hardly older than Aidan himself. The soldier's arms are wrapped tightly around himself and he's trembling violently. "Come on." Aidan extends a hand to the shivering soldier. "Get in. And then we're getting out of here as fast as we can."

NINE

Overhead, the planes have moved on and the bombs have stopped pelting down, but his heart is still racing—why have they stopped? What if they come back?

The soldier whom they've just picked up is seated next to Sally. He's got a blanket one of the other soldiers left behind wrapped around his shoulders and his shivering has stopped at least for the time being. Aidan turns away from them and focuses on steering the boat.

But a *thud* makes him turn sharply around. Sally's slipped off of the seat—that sound he heard was her body falling to the deck of the boat.

The soldier crouches next to her, shaking her shoulder until her eyes flutter open.

"What's wrong?" Aidan cries as he looks at her with alarm.

"I don't know . . ." Taking the hand the soldier has extended, Sally gets up off the deck and eases herself back into the seat. "I just feel very faint all of a sudden."

"When did you eat last?" asks the soldier.

"I don't remember," Sally says. "But not for a while. Certainly not since we left the village."

"But that was forever ago!" Aidan says. "Aren't you hungry?"

"I wasn't until this very second," she says. "But now that you mention it, I'm starving!"

"That can happen," the soldier tells her. "When you're in the thick of things, you don't feel hungry or thirsty. But that doesn't mean your body doesn't need to eat or drink. You should have something right away. You don't want to pass out again." He eyes Aidan for a second. "And something for you too—I'll bet you haven't eaten anything in a while either."

"But we don't have any food," Aidan says. "We left

in such a hurry that we didn't think to pack anything."

"Some of the others will," the soldier says. He stands up and waves to a man on a nearby boat. "Hey, mate," he calls out, "these two need some tea and whatever you've got on board. Can you spare something?"

"Of course we can!" the man calls back. "Just get a little closer."

Aidan brings the boat in and the soldier reaches for the parcel and the thermos that the man is offering. But Sally, who is clearly very weak, has slipped off the seat again. This time she doesn't come to right away.

"I think she's fainted!" Aidan says.

"Help me pick her up," says the soldier.

Aidan does as he's told, and together they prop Sally up. Her head lolls back and her hair is a wild mass of snarls.

"Better send her over to that boat," says the soldier. "It's bigger and she can lie down."

"But I don't want to be apart from her," Aidan says. "We came out here together and she's my best friend and . . ." He trails off, aware of how feeble this sounds. Sally does need help.

"I understand," says the soldier. "But she'll be better off. She's no help to you here and you can't do much for her either. You want her up and about again, don't you?"

"I suppose you're right," says Aidan. Sally would be more comfortable if she could stretch out, and the dory is too small.

"Can you take her?" the soldier asks the man in the other boat.

"Aye, we can," says the man. "My wife will look after her."

Aidan brings the dory very close and passes the anchor over, tethering the two vessels together. Then he and the soldier carefully lift Sally up and pass her over to the man and his wife, waiting on the other boat. Sally's body is as limp as a rag doll's.

When she's safely on the other boat, Aidan retrieves the anchor and turns to the parcel of food. He has no idea of what time it is, but he knows he's hungry. Ravenous, in fact. He unwraps the waxed paper to find a ham sandwich inside. He could inhale the whole thing in a single gulp but offers half to the soldier.

"You need it more, mate," he says, shaking his head. "But I'll take some of that tea."

Aidan unscrews the lid of the thermos and takes a swig. The tea isn't very warm, but it's sweet and strong and comforting nonetheless. Then he passes the thermos over to the soldier.

"My name's Ralph," says the soldier after he's had a drink and passed the thermos back.

"I'm Aidan." The words are a bit muffled because his mouth is filled with the sandwich. Has anything ever tasted so good? As he wolfs it down, he sees the boat that's carrying Sally moving away. He feels a sharp pang.

"She'll be all right," Ralph says, following his gaze.

"I hope so. She's been my best friend forever and we always stick together."

"Plucky girl, coming out here like this." He looks Aidan up and down. "You too—how old are you anyway?"

"Twelve."

Ralph nods. "Very brave, both of you. Do your mum and dad know you're here?"

"Yes."

"And they let you come out here by yourselves?"

"Not exactly . . ." Aidan tells Ralph about having to sneak out through the window.

"You really wanted to do your part!" exclaims Ralph.

"We both did." Again, Aidan's gaze turns in the direction of the boat that is taking Sally farther and farther from him.

"Well, I say that's noble," says Ralph, and exhausted as Aidan feels, pride covers him like a warm cloak. He's finished with the sandwich and begins rummaging around in the bag again. At the bottom, wrapped in another square of waxed paper, are a half dozen or so round McVitie's digestive biscuits. They're cracked but that doesn't matter a bit. He hands one to Ralph and they pass the thermos back and forth until the tea and the biscuits are gone.

After the meal is finished, Aidan feels much better and he starts up the engine once more. He decides he'll bring Ralph to a bigger boat that has just mercifully appeared and then find another soldier to ferry to safety. He has to stay busy, to keep his mind from worrying about George, who is out there somewhere, and Sally. Has she woken up yet?

He realizes that when he brings Ralph to the next boat, he's going to be all alone for the first time since he escaped from his bedroom. He's not sure how he feels about that—scared, for sure. But beneath the fear, there is a glowing little core of confidence too. He's come this far, hasn't he? Well, he won't stop now. He'll just keep on going until the job is done—because really, what else can he do?

TEN

George hates saying good bye to Aidan. To think that his little brother and neighbor had found the courage and resolve to take the *Margaret* and come out here by themselves—the very thought of it makes him choke up with pride.

But that pride is tempered by concern when he thinks about his parents. Mum and Dad must know that Aidan's gone by now, and if they know, they must be so worried. They've already lost one son to this terrible war. And now their two other boys are out here, facing untold dangers from the enemy that surrounds them. George has a moment of doubt—maybe he should have gone with Aidan and Sally. He could have looked out for them, and maybe kept them safe. But he knows that he had no real choice. This is about more than protecting his family—it's about protecting everyone: his unit and his town and his country.

Back on the shore, the jeep has driven off and Rogers is trying to make some kind of order out of the chaos. He's gotten the fleeing soldiers to line up two by two, so that the procession down to the water and into the boats will feel like an organized plan and not a stampede. For the most part, the men are obeying, but the air is thick with the soldiers' fear, and George is worried that they'll panic as soon as the German planes return.

Prompted by Rogers, George makes sure that the line is moving steadily. But what's going on over there? A big, burly fellow is trying to push ahead of the others. He elbows his way to the front of the line, and the other men shout at him as he shoves them aside.

George marches over to investigate. "There'll be none of that here," he says. "Go back to the end of the line and wait your turn like the rest of the men."

"You can't make me," says the big fellow. "You're not even in charge here."

"Yes, I am," says George, looking around for Rogers, who seems to have disappeared.

"Prove it," says the big fellow, who folds his arms across his chest and plants his enormous feet on the shore. His massive legs are like twin tree trunks and his muscles bulge under the sleeves of his uniform.

George doesn't know what to do. Rogers gave him orders and it's his duty to carry them out. He looks up at the man who is so defiant and uncooperative. What kind of soldier acts this way, ignoring the common good to put himself first? They are all working together toward the same goal—why can't the fellow see that?

Nervously, George looks around, hoping to gain support from the other soldiers. But they seem to be edging away from the brewing conflict. George doesn't want to fight the other man, who is taller and at least three stone heavier than he is, only he doesn't know what other choice he has.

But as George looks out across the water, scanning for his CO, he realizes that there is another even more pressing problem. There are only three boats out there—for what must be thirty-five or forty soldiers here, waiting to be carried back across the Channel. George can just make out the dory his father owns, the one with Aidan and Sally in it. But that's only big enough for a few men. The other two boats appear to be a bit larger, though not nearly large enough for the long line of men on the beach. No wonder that soldier tried to push ahead: He's frightened for his life and wants to be rescued. Pushing in front of the others is hardly a noble thing to do. Yet it's perfectly under-standable too. When George thinks of it that way, he manages to forgive the soldier.

But why is he wasting time thinking about this? If there aren't enough boats, none of these men will be saved, and they'll all perish—George included. The sol-diers are getting restless now. They must see that there are too many of them and too few boats. George is going to have to do something, and do it quickly.

"Now, look here, mate—" he starts to say, when a series of deafening booms drowns out all words. Blimey, it's Jerry and he's on the attack again! Almost from out of nowhere, bombs are raining down all around them, bright flashes that land in fiery plumes along the shore or in the water.

All pandemonium breaks loose and the men who were lined up for the places in the boats suddenly begin to scatter like rabbits, desperate to find places to hide. The man who tried to push ahead in line is leading the pack and in seconds, all the men have disappeared.

The boats have a harder time and George sees a boat directly in front of him take a terrible hit, the prow demolished in a blaze of flames. Amazingly enough, the *Margaret* is unscathed—at least for the moment.

The hideous sounds of screaming and blasts, the overpowering, acrid stench, the sky darkening from the thick coils of smoke rising slowly—George processes all this information in a matter of seconds. Yet he feels that time has frozen. Then his survival instinct kicks in. Like all those other men, he has to find a place to hide—*now*.

He begins running up the beach, but it's hard to breathe—the thick smoke clogging the air is making him gag and choke. Random fires have erupted everywhere and the shoreline is filled with debris of all kinds—George sees a couple of men lying on the ground—Wounded? Dead?—before he forces himself to stop looking altogether and to keep his gaze straight ahead, intent on finding shelter.

He runs up the beach, away from the shoreline and toward a cluster of small brick buildings that are set back behind some shrubs. As he nears them, he spies a pair of red cellar doors, their battered silver handles gleaming like a beacon. A cellar is a good place to be during an air strike. A relatively safe place.

Wheezing with exertion, he rushes for the doors. He's almost there, reaching for the handle, when a bomb explodes somewhere close behind him. He doesn't see it, but he can feel the powerful impact, the heat, and then the horrible pain that comes when a piece of shrapnel, red-hot and burning, flies from the blast and lodges deeply in his thigh. Clutching the wound, he crumples to the ground before everything goes mercifully black.

Aidan is still alone in the dory when the bombs start raining down again. He is frightened, more frightened than he's ever been in his entire life, and he can feel his body trembling each time a bomb hits the water. A boat right next to him is destroyed, right before his eyes. He is frozen in shock and horror, so he is scarcely aware of the other boats in the water.

"Get in!" calls a woman. "Now!"

Her voice breaks the trance and Aidan looks up to see that another boat has pulled in close beside the *Margaret*. He scrambles aboard and takes cover with the woman and the man who is with her.

"Out here all by yourself, are you?" she asks. She wears a checked kerchief over her graying hair, and her brown eyes are kind.

"I wasn't alone when I came," Aidan says. "I was here with my friend Sally and I found my brother

George too, only—" His words are swallowed up in another screaming blast from the sky above.

Instinctively, Aidan drops to his knees and tucks his chin close to his chest. The woman puts an arm around his shoulders and even though she's a perfect stranger, he feels enormously comforted by the small gesture.

"There, there," she says when the noise has passed. "Put this on, why don't you?" Aidan sees she has handed him a life vest. She and the man, who must be her husband, are both wearing them.

"All right." He slips his arms through the holes. It's a bit big but there's a belt at the waist and he cinches it as tightly as he can.

The water is quiet for the moment, though there are still planes in the sky, hovering ominously above them. Following the direction of Aidan's gaze, the woman looks upward. "Let's all go belowdecks until Jerry gets tired of dropping things on us," she says.

Aidan follows her and her husband belowdecks, where they remain for a while. The sound of the bombs is muffled down here and because Aidan's so very exhausted, the gentle rocking of the boat almost lulls him to sleep. He closes his eyes. *Just for a minute,* he thinks. *Just for one little minute.*

His mind drifts and for a few amazing seconds, he actually sleeps, even in the midst of the terror surrounding him. But with sleep comes the dream—the wall of water, black and terrifying, rising above him and blotting out the sun and the sky.

The dream wave breaks just as another bomb crashes down. His eyes fly open and he gasps as he plunges into the icy gray water. This bomb must have hit the deck directly, because suddenly there is no boat, no woman, and no husband either, just the charred wreckage bobbing around him.

Flailing around in the churning sea, Aidan feels the cold water invade his nose, mouth, and lungs. Just as in the dream, he's going to drown, even though it's the wake of a bomb and not a tidal wave that's going to deliver the fatal blow. But then something in him, some instinctive fighting spirit, takes hold and he kicks frantically to the surface. Once his head has emerged, he coughs, sputters, sending the water out and allowing him to take in the air again.

He won't go down without a struggle—he won't. He tries to remain calm, to think of his father's face, his father's voice. And he remembers the things his father said when they went out fishing together. "The important thing about going overboard is not to panic," his father said. "Panic wastes energy, and you need every single bit of it."

Aidan takes a deep breath and tries to do what his father said. He stops struggling and instead uses his energy to tread water, careful to keep his head clear of the choppy waves. He doesn't see the woman and man who rescued him, but he can see the dory, empty now, some distance away. He's trying to figure out whether he can swim to it, when a piece of the destroyed boat floats past him and he reaches out to grab it with both hands.

Once Aidan's got something to cling to, it's easier to relax. Between the piece of wood, which is large enough to hold on to, and the life vest, he can afford to ease up on the constant motion of treading water and catch his breath.

Only, now that he's not moving, he's keenly aware of how cold the water feels. Even though it's May, the sea has hardly warmed up at all. His teeth begin to chatter and his legs start to cramp up from the chill. Maybe he should start treading water again, even if not so desperately—the constant motion will keep him from feeling the cold.

But when he starts to move his arms and legs, a strong wave comes along and bats the piece of the boat right out of his hands. He actually utters a little cry when he sees it carried swiftly away, out of reach and soon out of sight.

Aidan's spirits are at their lowest ever. Yes, he still has the life vest, but it's no protection against the drop ping temperature. And though he's long since lost track of the time, he can see the sun dipping lower in the sky. Soon it will be pitch-black, and he'll be out here alone. He thinks of his parents, frantically calling him back as he and Sally sped away. Where are they now? And what's become of Sally and George? He'll never know, just like they'll never know what happened to him. They'll only know that he met his end during this terrible day, but not when, where, or how.

This thought is so painful that Aidan wants to yell out loud, a heartfelt scream to let loose all that he's feeling. Well, why not? Who'll hear him anyway? He utters a low, guttural sound at first, and then his voice grows louder, and louder still. The bombs have stopped now, and he can hear his own anguished cry rising above the waves.

Then, to his astonishment, he hears a sound in reply. Or does he? Maybe he's just dreaming, imagining a rescue that will never come. He lets out another resounding scream. This time, the response is clear and definite.

"Ahoy!" calls a man's voice. "Is anyone there?"

"Yes, I'm here! Over here!" Aidan shoots a hand up and waves it frantically, trying to peer in the direction of the voice. It's coming from a boat, a small blue-and-white craft with oars—it reminds him of Mr. Potts's boat from his village. And when he looks again, he sees another boat and then another and another—a whole fleet! Where are they coming from?

Aidan swims in the direction of the blue-and-white boat—it's the closest—and when he reaches the side, a strong pair of arms reaches down to pull him from the water's embrace and onto the safety of the deck. He remains there for a few seconds, still shivering and panting hard, before he looks up to see the face of his rescuer. When he does, he is dumbstruck. The man looking down at him with such concern and love is none other than his father.

ELEVEN

When George opens his eyes he doesn't know where he is, or how he got there. He barely even knows *who* he is—all he knows is pain, and his entire consciousness is focused on that. The pain in his leg has somehow radiated out, enveloping his whole body. He's never experienced anything like it before.

"Hey, I think he's coming round," says a voice somewhere above him.

"Water," says another voice. "Get him some water and be quick about it."

There is some movement and then a tin cup of water is lifted to George's lips. He doesn't realize how cracked and dry they are until he runs his tongue across them, nor how parched he's feeling until the water slides down his throat.

"Thank you," he says. Or tries to say. His voice is the merest whisper, and even uttering those faint words feels like a huge accomplishment.

There's something hovering above his face and he squints in concentration, trying to make sense of it. It's a face—and not just any face. Miraculously enough, it's the face of his CO.

"Hey, mate, glad you're still with us," says Rogers. "It was touch and go for a while."

"Where am I?" he manages to croak out before he has to close his eyes again.

"Down here in the cellar. You were trying to reach it when you were hit."

Hit. Yes, so that was what happened. George remembers the frantic scramble up the beach, and the pair of red doors that he was seeking before the pain came and obliterated everything else.

"We heard you out there and came to get you. Good thing too—another bomb hit just after they brought you down. If you'd still been out there, you'd have been a goner for sure."

Eyes still closed, George nods, and soon he drifts back into a light sleep. The pain is still with him, setting off sparks that sizzle and burn in his leg, points of heat that radiate throughout his body. When he wakes, he sees another face hovering close. This one is unfamiliar.

"Now, this may hurt," says the man who is above him.

This *may* hurt? If he had the energy, George would laugh. Everything hurts. Why doesn't this fool know that?

The man is doing something to his leg. Something that *hurts*.

"Got it!" The man, who turns out to be a medic, raises a jagged piece of metal in the air with what appears to be a giant pair of tweezers. "Now let me bandage you up."

Water, ointment, gauze . . . and then George's head is gently lifted from the floor and a large pill is placed under his tongue. The tin cup reappears.

"Swallow it down," says the medic. "It'll help with the pain."

George does as he's told and to his vast relief, he drifts off into sleep again. His dreams are busy and chaotic but the thread of them remains the same—he's looking for his brother Aidan. If only he could find him . . .

"Dad!" exclaims Aidan. "What's going on? How did you get here?"

"You're all right, thank God you're all right!"

Aidan turns to see that his mother has appeared right beside his father.

"I don't understand," he says as his mother wraps her arms around him in a fierce hug. "But maybe it doesn't matter—I'm just so glad you're here!"

"It's because of you," his mother says as she wipes the tears—of joy and relief, he knows—from her face. "You and Sally."

"What do you mean?" Aidan asks.

"After the two of you ran off, Mum and I didn't know what to do," his father says. "We were so worried.

So upset. Then the answer came to us, clear as a bell. If you two youngsters were brave enough to go, why, then we had to go too. And so did all our neighbors. Those people at the town hall meeting the other night? Everyone who had a boat decided to go. Every last man and woman."

"That's right," his mum adds. "When we told everyone what you'd done, they all wanted to join in. Why, practically the whole village is here—just look around you."

Aidan raises his head to glance about and sees that his mother is right. There are so many boats he recognizes from the village, like Ned Blarry's and Herb Whitson's. And this boat he's crouched in right now— he knows this one too. "Doesn't this boat belong to Mr. Potts?" Mr. Potts lives by himself in a cottage near the edge of the village. He has white hair and a full white beard. He'd been a fisherman years ago, but he's long since retired from the sea.

"It does indeed," says his father. "He's got the arthritis so bad he couldn't join in, but when I told him what we were doing, he offered the *Evening Star* straightaway. You see, you and Sally set an example for the whole town. Your bravery and selflessness inspired others to do the same—so many others." His father gestures to the boats that dot the water.

But Aidan's mind is elsewhere. Sally. Just hearing her name causes a pit of fear to open in his stomach. "Where is Sally?" he asks. "She fainted a while ago and we moved her to another boat. I haven't seen her since. Is she all right?"

There is a weighty silence during which his parents exchange looks. The pit of fear in Aidan's stomach gapes wider. "What is it?" he demands. "What's happened to her? You have to tell me!"

"That boat she was on—" his father says.

"You mean the one I put her on!" Aidan bursts out. If something's happened to Sally, he's to blame because he was the one who agreed to move her.

"Yes, that one," his father says. "Well, it's like this . . ." He seems to be searching for the words. "It was hit, you see. The boat took a direct hit. And Sally was hurt in the explosion."

"Oh no," Aidan says, covering his face with his hands so no one will see the scalding tears that leap into his eyes. "No, no, no!"

His father puts one hand on his shoulder but Aidan twitches it off. He doesn't deserve his father's comfort now—not after what he's done. Finally, he lifts up his face and asks, "Where is she now?"

"She's here," his mother says. "We found her in the water and we brought her aboard. She's belowdecks."

"Can I see her?" Aidan asks.

Again the silence.

"There's not enough room right now," his father says. "Her folks are down there with her, and so is Nora Billingham." Nora Billingham is the nurse in their village. "Best to wait until they come up."

"All right." Aidan paces back and forth on the deck. At last, Mr. and Mrs. Sparks emerge from below. They look very anxious and Mrs. Sparks's eyes are red and teary.

Aidan says hello to them and then turns to his father. "Now can I see her? Please?"

"All right," he says at last. "Your mum will go down with you. But you may want to brace yourself first. She . . . well, it looks pretty bad."

"That doesn't matter. I've got to see her anyway," Aidan insists. He turns to face his mother. "Please," he says. "Can you take me to her now?"

TWELVE

Using a sturdy tree branch as an improvised cane, George limps his way down to the shore. The bombing has stopped, at least for the time being, and since the coast is clear, Rogers has decided they'll head back to the water. With the whole town under attack, it's too dangerous to remain in the cellar. So it's back to the boats—that is, if there are any boats left.

George doesn't know what time it is but it's almost dark. All around, he can see the results of the recent bombing. Buildings are aflame, wreckage is everywhere, and the dead lie still and silent. George's heart aches to see them, the valiant men who've fallen trying to ward off the Nazi menace.

Then George stops. There, lying right in front of him, is the big, belligerent soldier who was giving him such a hard time just hours ago. Silently, George says a little prayer for the dead man, and then another of thanksgiving that his own wound, painful as it is, came in the leg. He is lucky that the shrapnel didn't hit his face or some vital organ.

Tears rise in his eyes as he continues down toward the beach. The soldier wanted to live, that's all. Just to get home safely. The tears now cloud his vision and he has to wipe them away before he can go on.

When George can see clearly again, it's as if a miracle is taking place before his eyes. Earlier, there were only three boats in the water. Now there must be more than a dozen. And what's more, he knows them; he recognizes them. These are the little boats from his village, owned by people he's known his entire life. But how did this happen? Who brought them all here?

Hurrying as best he can on his wounded leg, George stands at the shoreline, water lapping at the toes of his combat boots. The dory is nowhere to be seen, and George feels a stab of fear. If the dory is gone, where are Aidan and Sally? He scans the horizon anxiously, and to his relief, he sees the dory. It was hidden behind a larger boat. This boat is blue and white and George knows it at once. This is the boat that belongs to old Mr. Potts, who had been in the navy before becoming a fisherman.

As a small boy, George was allowed to explore that boat. It was much bigger than the dory and had living quarters down below—two narrow beds, a table, and two benches. Once, George was invited to spend the night and he thought it was the most exciting thing ever. Mr. Potts kept him up until all hours spinning wild yarns about his life at sea—storms, pirates, whales, and even a mermaid or two. George knew that these stories were largely made up, but that didn't stop him from enjoying them immensely. Yes, that's Potts's boat, all right—George is certain of it.

He wades into the shallow water, eyes trained on the blue-and-white boat. Standing at the wheel is a man in a sweater and tweed cap, but the man is younger than Mr. Potts. In fact, he looks a lot like George's father.

George wades out deeper and deeper, the water chilly and biting as it swirls around his knees. Soon the water splashes up even higher, wetting the fabric of his jacket. His wound starts to throb, but George scarcely notices. That man is his father, yes he is!

"Dad!" he cries, waving with a single hand at the boat. "Dad, it's me—George!"

Aidan follows his mum down the few steps that lead belowdecks. Sally is on a narrow bed under a blue blanket, a bandage wrapped around her head, her eyes closed. Nurse Billingham is seated on one bench, shaking the mercury down in a glass thermometer.

"Hello, Aidan," she says softly. Her bun has come loose and there are deep shadows under her eyes.

"How is she?" Aidan asks, not sure if he really wants to hear the truth.

"Well, she took a blow to the head and she wasn't conscious when we found her. I've patched her up as best I can, but it's hard to tell. If she comes to, we'll know she can pull out of it. If she doesn't . . ."

Aidan doesn't need her to finish the sentence. "Can I talk to her?" he asks.

"Of course," Nurse Billingham says. "I don't know that she'll be able to hear you but it can't hurt to try. Her mum was singing to her just a little while ago."

Aidan approaches the bed nervously. Sally is pale and still and he finds himself looking very hard to see if she is even breathing. He is relieved when he can see the slight movement her chest makes, up and down, up and down.

"Hey, Sally," he says. "I'm sorry you got hurt. So sorry."

There is no reply.

"But you're a fighter," he continues. "You always were. You can fight your way out of this one, Sally. I know you can."

Aidan waits for her to give some indication she's

heard him, even a flicker of her eyes. But she remains silent and motionless. Finally, he turns away.

"Try not to take it too hard," Nurse Billingham says. "Maybe she'll pull through." But she doesn't sound confident.

"Maybe?" Aidan says. "That's all—just maybe?"

"It's the best I can do now, lad," she says. "Why don't you go up and see your dad? He's been so worried about you. I'll stay down here and if there's any change, I'll pop right up and tell you about it."

Aidan hesitates and she adds, "You can trust me." So, sighing deeply, he climbs the stairs. If Sally doesn't pull through, he knows he'll never forgive himself. He's the one who brought her into this. If it hadn't been for him, she'd be safe at home.

Up on deck, Aidan sees that night has fallen, and lights from the boats gleam ominously on the oil-slick water. The boat is moving quickly toward the shoreline, probably to pick up some of the soldiers who are now lining up on the beach. But there is one soldier moving out into the water. He appears to have been hurt because he's clearly unsteady on his feet and is using some kind of cane. It seems very risky for him to be wading out into the water. Why doesn't he remain safely on the shore with the others? Someone ought to make sure he gets back onto solid ground.

Aidan hears his dad choke out a sob and runs up next to him at the helm.

"Dad! Over here, Dad!" the soldier is shouting, and his father uses one hand to steer while he waves the other up in the air. "George!" cries his father. "George, don't take another step! We're coming—you wait right where you are!"

Aidan leans out over the prow. George! They've found George and this time they're going to take him home! The boat comes closer and closer and as soon as it is close enough, Aidan reaches down to help his father pull George aboard.

They're all weeping and hugging, and their mum is covering George's face with hundreds of kisses.

"You're limping," she says when she finally steps back for a moment. "You've been hurt."

"Aye, but not too badly," says George. "Shrapnel got me in the leg but the piece is out now. I'll be as good as new soon."

Aidan is relieved to hear it but the relief sours quickly when he thinks of Sally, lying there belowdecks. Will she ever be as good as new? He tries to push the thought away, to just let himself feel glad about his brother. George is here, safe and sound. At least he can be thankful for that.

"Where did all these boats come from?" George looks around. "Practically the whole village is here." When his eyes come to rest on Mr. and Mrs. Sparks, he hobbles over to give them a hug.

"It's true," says their dad. "And it's really because of Aidan and Sally. When I told everyone how they'd run off to come over here, everyone who was on the fence wanted to come and help too."

"Where is Sally?" George asks.

Aidan finds the words are frozen in his mouth and he can't say them. He just looks down, unable to meet his brother's eyes.

"She was hurt," Mrs. Sparks says for him. "She's belowdecks now. We're all praying for her. Let's do it together, shall we?"

For a moment, they all close their eyes and join hands in a silent prayer. Aidan prays harder than he ever has in his life. *Please let her be all right. Please, please, please.*

Aidan opens his eyes when the hands holding his let go. The boats of the village are all around, and soldiers are making their way on board the different vessels. With all the recently arrived boats, it looks like there will be room for everyone. Aidan's heart swells with relief and happiness—they're going to be saved. Every single man here will be saved. If only Sally knew! She'd be as happy and proud as he is.

Not saying a word to anyone, Aidan heads for the steps. But belowdecks there is no change in Sally. Nurse Billingham has stretched out on the other bed and closed her eyes. She looked awfully tired earlier, and Aidan takes care not to disturb her.

Silently, he tiptoes over to Sally's bed and takes her

cold, clammy hand in his. Then he bends down and whispers urgently in her ear. "We did it, Sally. We really, truly did it. If only you'd open your eyes, you wouldn't believe what you would see. The whole village is here—your mum and dad, and mine too. They all came, and there's room for all the men now. They're coming home, Sally. We're bringing them home."

Aidan stares at his friend, willing her to wake up. Her eyes remain closed and her chest continues its rhythmic rise and fall. He squeezes her hand just a bit harder. "Oh, Sally, please won't you wake up? Do it for me, Sally. Please do it for me. I know you can."

And then, to his amazement, there is a flickering of her eyelids. Or does he just think he sees it because it's what he so badly wants to see? "Sally," he repeats. "Sally, open your eyes."

And just like that, she does.

Her gaze skitters around the room at first and she seems confused until she sees Aidan's face. "There you are!" she says, and her lips, which are dry and chapped, form a smile. "I was dreaming about you, Aidan.

Such a good dream. We'd saved all the boys, every last one of them. And I was so happy."

"It's not just a dream!" he cries. "It's true! And we've found George again! He's wounded but he's going to be fine, perfectly fine. When you're strong enough, you'll come up the stairs on deck and you'll see for yourself!" He's afraid to hug her, but he continues to clutch her hand and they sit like that for several seconds, just beaming at each other.

Then Nurse Billingham wakes up and her face breaks into a wide smile when she sees that Sally is awake. "Why, it's just a day filled with miracles, isn't it?" she says as she joins Aidan at Sally's bedside. "Miracles all around."

Then she turns to Sally. "Welcome back, lass," she says. "We were worried about you, but since you're up, I think you're through the worst of it. Now how about a spot of tea?"

THIRTEEN

George sleeps most of the way back across the Channel. He is exhausted from the stress of this long and harrowing day, and from all the long, harrowing days that came before. And the shrapnel wound still hurts. Nurse Billingham applies a salve to the spot and that makes it feel a little better, but he is relieved he can go home. He'll return to active combat when he is feeling stronger and his leg is fully healed.

It's still dark when the *Evening Star* arrives in the village, but by the time everyone is off the boat and they're back at the cottage, the first faint streaks of dawn are lighting the sky.

Exhausted, relieved, joyful, and filled with gratitude, George tumbles into his own bed for the first time in months. Here's the familiar blue comforter, and the red-green-blue afghan Mum knit one year for Christmas. On the wall is the chart of the periodic table he tacked up, as well as the poster that shows all the musculature in the human body. He deliberately doesn't look at the other side of the room, where Trevor's neatly made bed remains just as it was, or at what his brother chose to hang above it: a poster advertising the circus and another for a popular musical that played in London. Trevor didn't make it home. George did. And so did Aidan. There's no rhyme or reason to any of it, and George isn't going to spend another second trying to make sense of what's unfolded. Instead, he closes his eyes against the brightening day, and sleeps for nearly twenty straight hours.

George spends a lot of time reading and just taking it easy, but after a few days, he finds himself getting restless. He starts taking daily walks down to the water, happy to be back on English soil and to stand on the dock, looking at all the brave little boats that crossed the sea and brought him and the other boys home. Many of them had never been in open water before, and the men and women who steered them weren't enlisted soldiers or trained for their mission. They had just seen the need and heeded the call. Their heroism makes George grateful and proud. It also makes him eager to return to combat—the war is far from over, and every man is needed to fight against the ruthless enemy.

"Don't rush back," says his mum. "You've got to be well first."

"Mum's right," adds his dad. "We need strong, battle-ready boys. You'll be of greater use to the country if you get your strength up before you go back."

One day shortly before he is ready to return to active duty, George is sorting through his things when he pulls out the wallet he picked up from the dead German soldier. The two pictures, the ID card, the money, and even the frayed bit of ribbon—it feels like a year since he first looked through, but everything he remembers is still there. He wonders if he could find

Gerhardt's parents to return it to them. Would they want to have this back again? Or would receiving it make them too sad?

Then his thoughts turn to his own parents. Would his mum and dad want to receive such a package from the soldier who killed his brother? He doesn't know the answer to those questions. Besides, he doesn't have any idea of how he might track down Gerhardt's parents. And even if he did, would a letter or package to a German family even get delivered when Britain and Germany are fierce enemies? Probably not, and then the wallet would end up discarded, like so much trash.

No, he decides, he won't try to return the wallet. It's better to keep it himself, so it will be respected and protected. The wallet will also serve as a reminder of the price of war.

George thinks of the men he's known who have died, some of whom were friends, and others whose names he'd never even known. He still believes in his country and the necessity of fighting the Nazis. Hitler's goal is world domination—he's come out and said so, over and over again. To George, there is no choice—the evil dictator must be stopped. And yet this German soldier, and all the others, had to die because of one man's murderous aims . . .

George puts the wallet in a locked box of special things he keeps under his bed. The wallet, the final record of a young man who was born in Germany and died in France—that will be George's forever, something to pass on to his son or even his grandson, along with the story of how he came to own it.

He fastens the lock and tucks the key under a loose floorboard in a far corner of the room. *Rest in peace*, he says silently, not just to Gerhardt, but to his brother and all the other fallen boys. He'll think of them when he's back in the thick of things. Think of them—and strive always to be courageous, to honor their sacred memory.

Aidan and Sally are treated as heroes when they come home—even more than Mrs. McAllister's rousing speech, the story of how these two young people put themselves in grave danger encouraged the whole village to turn out for their boys. There's a special assembly at school, and a party at the local tea shop, at which several officials make speeches and shake their hands. A photographer and reporter are there too, and their picture ends up on the front page of the local paper.

All told, over three hundred thousand soldiers, British, French, and Belgian, were saved by the evacuation—three hundred thousand young men who lived to tell the tale of their harrowing adventure and returned to continue the fight.

"I was scared," Aidan confesses to Sally. Well after the party has ended, they are sitting in the room at the top of the lighthouse. "So scared."

"Scared?" says Sally. "I was terrified. But somehow we got through anyway, didn't we?"

"We certainly did."

They sit in silence for a moment, musing about their adventure. Sally's still wearing a bandage on her head, though she's feeling stronger every day. Still, Nurse Billingham has warned her against doing anything even remotely dangerous, including riding a bicycle.

Aidan looks out at the sea, which is a steel blue with foamy, white-capped waves today. He likes being able to see out so far—there are fishing boats, a couple of rowboats, and even a sailboat, though he doesn't recognize whose it is. Everything seems peaceful and safe, but he knows it's just an illusion. Yes, these vessels and others like them have succeeded in bringing the boys back home, but the war is far from over. There's still fighting on the Continent, and some people say it's only just getting started.

"George is going back to the front soon," he says.

"How soon?" Sally asks.

"Tomorrow, I think."

Sally is quiet for a moment before saying, "Your mum and dad—they must be very worried."

He nods. "They are, my mum especially. But they know he has to go."

"And you know that too, right?" asks Sally.

"Just like all the other courageous boys who go." Aidan continues to look out at the water. There's no controlling it, he realizes. The waves rise and fall, the tides go in and out, all governed by their own laws. It's *just like the war,* he thinks. There's no controlling what happens on the battlefield or in the air. War has no laws, no logic. The outcome is uncertain. "Anyway, we proved a thing or two, didn't we?" he asks her.

"I suppose we did. We showed the whole village that being afraid wasn't enough of a reason not to do something."

Aidan knows that *he's* less afraid now than he once was. That dream about the wall of water? He's had it only once since his return to the village. And to his amazement, the ending was different. Though the wave in the dream crashed over him, he wasn't sucked under to drown like his poor brother. Instead, he popped up on the other side of it, bobbing lightly in the undertow, like a piece of cork. "The goodwill of all those other people, our mums and dads, and ordinary people just like them—just like us—really makes a difference," he says.

"Yes, it does," Sally says.

"George says that in some ways, the war is just beginning," says Aidan. "And I think he's right. But if everyone pulls together, like we did, well then, maybe we'll win." He turns away from the water to look at Sally. "Yes, I really believe that we will."

GLOSSARY OF TERMS

Since it's safe to say none of you have been to England during the 1940s, you might not know some common British slang and expressions.

BEF—British Expeditionary Force
Blighty—Nickname for England
Clobber—Slang for duffel bag and clothing
Clove hitch—A type of sailor's knot
CO—Commanding officer
Daft—Common British term meaning "crazy" or "mad"
Debus—Get off of a bus or truck
Football—The British use this term for the game we call soccer
Jerry—Slang for German soldier
Petrol—Gasoline
RAF—Royal Air Force, the airborne division of the British army
Stone—British measure of weight equal to about fourteen pounds
Tommy—Slang term for a British soldier
Union Jack—Name for the flag of England

BRIEF HISTORY OF WORLD WAR II

The official start of World War II was on September 1, 1939, when German troops invaded Poland. Germany was led by Adolf Hitler, who was also the head of the Nazi party. Under Hitler's leadership, the Nazis were intent on destroying groups they saw as inferior: mainly the Jewish people, but also other minorities such as Roma, homosexuals, and people with physical and developmental disabilities. Anyone who opposed the Nazi regime was also considered an enemy and was subject to imprisonment, punishment, or even death.

Great Britain and France responded to this attack on Poland by declaring war on Germany. Soon other countries joined in on either side of the conflict. The war was fought between the Axis powers (chiefly Germany, Italy, and Japan) and the Allied forces (chiefly Great Britain, the Soviet Union, and France).

At first, the United States resisted getting involved in the conflict, but on December 7, 1941, Japanese fighter planes bombed the naval base at Pearl Harbor in Hawaii. The attack occurred on a Sunday morning and caught the men completely by surprise. After this, the United States felt compelled to declare war on Japan and joined the war effort alongside the Allied Powers.

At first, the fighting was contained in Europe, but it soon spread throughout the world. Most battles took place in Europe, Southeast Asia, and the Pacific Ocean. It was the deadliest war in all of human history—around fifty million people were killed and many more were wounded.

At first it looked as if the Germans would win the war, and the fighting was long and bloody. Eventually, the tide turned and even Germany's allies, the Italians, turned against them. On April 30, 1945, Hitler committed suicide in his hidden bunker. Germany surrendered on May 7, 1945, and the war in Europe officially ended.

But the war continued in Asia, and did not end until the Americans dropped atomic bombs on Hiroshima and Nagasaki in August 1945. The war in the Pacific finally ended when Japan surrendered on August 14, 1945.

Time Line of WWII in England*

1939

- Hitler invades Poland on September 1. **Britain and France declare war on Germany two days later.**

1940

- **Rationing starts in the UK.**
- German "Blitzkrieg" overwhelms Belgium, Holland, and France.
- **Winston Churchill becomes prime minister of Britain.**
- **British Expeditionary Force evacuated from Dunkirk.**
- **British victory in Battle of Britain forces Hitler to postpone invasion plans.**

*Events that involve Britain are in boldface.

1941

- Hitler begins Operation Barbarossa—the invasion of the Soviet Union.
- **The Blitz continues against Britain's major cities.**
- Allies take Tobruk in North Africa and resist German attacks.
- Japan attacks Pearl Harbor, and the US enters the war.

1942

- Germany suffers setbacks at Stalingrad and El Alamein.
- Singapore falls to the Japanese in February— around 25,000 prisoners taken.
- American naval victory at Battle of Midway, in June, marks turning point in the Pacific war.
- Mass murder of Jewish people at Auschwitz begins.

1943

- Surrender at Stalingrad marks Germany's first major defeat.
- Allied victory in North Africa enables invasion of Italy to be launched.
- Italy surrenders, but Germany takes over the battle.
- **British and Indian forces fight Japanese in Burma.**

1944

- Allies land at Anzio and bomb monastery at Monte Cassino.
- Soviet offensive gathers pace in Eastern Europe.
- D-Day: The Allied invasion of France. Paris is liberated in August.
- Guam liberated by the US; Okinawa and Iwo Jima bombed.

1945

- Auschwitz liberated by Soviet troops.
- Soviets reach Berlin: Hitler commits suicide and Germany surrenders on May 7.
- Atomic bombs are dropped on Hiroshima and Nagasaki; Japan surrenders on August 14.

TIME LINE OF THE EVACUATION
OF DUNKIRK

In my fictional telling of this story, I tried to remain as close to the actual time line as possible. But since the events described here are not actual history, I took some liberties so I could move back and forth between Aidan's viewpoint and his brother George's. I also deliberately didn't use the name of an actual English village along the coast so that I could be free to let the story go where it took me.

May 20, 1940 Sensing an imminent and devastating loss, British prime minister Winston Churchill orders the preparation of vessels to evacuate the British Expeditionary Force from northern France.

May 20, 1940 Major battlefield losses across France and the Low Countries force a change in leadership, and Allied commander General Maurice-Gustave Gamelin is replaced by General Maxime Weygand.

May 24, 1940   Adolf Hitler orders his forces not to cross the Lens–Bethune–St-Omer–Gravelines line, which allows the retreating Allied forces more time to reach the French coast.

May 24, 1940   German Luftwaffe bombs Allied defensive positions in and around the French port city of Dunkirk.

May 25, 1940   The German army takes Boulogne, which is in France. More and more retreating Allied units arrive in Dunkirk.

May 26, 1940   Hitler orders his army forces toward Dunkirk to deliver the final blow to the Allied cause.

May 26, 1940   At 6:57 p.m., Operation Dynamo, the all-out evacuation of Allied forces from Dunkirk, officially begins. Over 850 civilian vessels take part in helping military forces from France to awaiting transports.

May 28, 1940 The Belgian army surrenders to the Germans. This buys the Allies time, and by the end of the day, 25,473 British soldiers have been evacuated from France.

May 29, 1940 Another 47,000 British troops are evacuated from Dunkirk.

May 30, 1940 Around 6,000 French soldiers join the 120,000 total Allied soldiers evacuated from Dunkirk on this day.

May 31, 1940 Over 150,000 Allied soldiers (including 15,000 who are French) arrive in Britain.

June 4, 1940 German Luftwaffe bombers end their bombing of Dunkirk.

Operation Dynamo, the largest military evacuation in history, officially ends: 338,326 soldiers are saved, including 113,000 French troops.

BIBLIOGRAPHY

Borden, Louise, and Michael Foreman (Illustrator).
1997. *The Little Ships: The Heroic Rescue at Dunkirk
in World War II*. New York: Margaret K.
McElderry Books.

Bowen, R. Sidney. 1941. *Dave Dawson at Dunkirk*. New
York: Crown Publishers.

Holland, James. 2011. *Duty Calls: Dunkirk*. New York:
Puffin Books.

Jackson, Robert. 1976. *Dunkirk: The British Evacuation,
1940*. London: Cassell.

Lord, Walter. 1982. *The Miracle of Dunkirk: The True
Story of Operation Dynamo*. New York: Viking.

Sebag-Montefiore, Hugh. 2006. *Dunkirk: Fight to the
Last Man*. Cambridge: Harvard University Press.

ACKNOWLEDGMENTS

I would like to thank my wonderful agent, Susanna Einstein, for—oh, just about *everything*, and Erin Black, whose stellar editorial eye turned the manuscript I handed her into the very best book it could be. Also thanks to Brooke Shearouse, Michelle Campbell, and the rest of the fabulous crew at Scholastic—your support has meant the world to me and I'm so grateful and proud to have found a home with you.

ABOUT THE AUTHOR

Yona Zeldis McDonough is the award-winning author of twenty-eight books for children and seven novels for adults. Her essays, articles, and short fiction have appeared in numerous national and literary publications. She is also the fiction editor of *Lilith* magazine. McDonough lives in Brooklyn with her husband.